Everyone loves us. The teachers like us .... work hard, and we're clever, polite and helpful. The other kids like us because we're pretty and popular and funny and smart. They even have a name for us. The Bindi Babes. No one's got more designer labels than we have. We've got everything we could ever want. Almost everything.

www.narinderdhami.com

Coming soon from Narinder Dhami:

BOLLYWOOD BABES

BINDI BABES

BABES

NARINDER DHAMI

CORGI YEARLING BOOKS

BINDI BABES
A CORGI YEARLING BOOK 0440 86512 3

Published in Great Britain by Corgi Books,
an imprint of Random House Children's Books

This edition published 2003

5 7 9 10 8 6

Papers used by Random House Children's Books are natural,
recyclable products made from wood grown in sustainable forests.
The manufacturing processes conform to the environmental regulations
of the country of origin.

Set in Palatino by
Palimpsest Book Production Limited, Polmont, Stirlinghsire

Corgi Books are published by Random House Children's Books,
61–63 Uxbridge Road, London W5 5SA,
a division of The Random House Group Ltd,
in Australia by Random House Australia (Pty) Ltd,
20 Alfred Street, Milsons Point, Sydney, NSW 2061, Australia,
in New Zealand by Random House New Zealand Ltd,
18 Poland Road, Glenfield, Auckland 10, New Zealand,
and in South Africa by Random House (Pty) Ltd,
Endulini, 5A Jubilee Road, Parktown 2193, South Africa

THE RANDOM HOUSE GROUP Limited Reg. No. 954009
www.kidsatrandomhouse.co.uk

A CIP catalogue record for this book is available from the British Library.

Printed and bound in Great Britain by
Bookmarque Ltd, Croydon, Surrey

For Bambi and Sue,
my sisters and best friends

CHAPTER 1

Once upon a time there were three sisters called Geena, Amber and Jazz. I'm Amber, the best looking and certainly the most intelligent. When the other two have finished killing me, I'll tell you what happened to us.

Our story's got something of everything, just like a Bollywood movie. It's got singing, dancing, action, romance, a baddie and three beautiful heroines.

The story begins on the day my so-called friend, Kim, got stuck up a ladder. It was also the day our lives changed for ever.

It begins at lunch time. Lunch time at Coppergate Secondary School was a take-your-life-in-your-hands kind of affair. The canteen was falling down, so it was always possible that a lump of plaster would drop from the ceiling into your apple pie and custard at any moment. To be honest, the whole of the lower school was falling down. The upper seniors had already moved into a state-of-the-art new building across the road, but we had to wait for the rest of it to be built.

'I'm getting new trainers,' I told my friends Chelsea and Sharelle. We were sitting in the playground after lunch, giving the boys marks out of ten for looks and style.

'New trainers!' Sharelle shrieked. 'If you tell me you're getting those silver Reeboks with the high-tech soles for smoother movement, and laces guaranteed for life, I'm going to die.'

'I am,' I said.

Sharelle turned visibly green. It could have been the fish pie we had for lunch, but I didn't think so. I liked it when people were envious. It meant they weren't pitying me.

'You're so lucky, Amber Dhillon,' Chelsea moaned. 'You get everything you want.'

'Not everything,' I said meaningfully.

Chelsea and Sharelle looked embarrassed.

'Well, most things,' Chelsea said hurriedly. 'Has Geena got a new phone?'

Geena was across the playground, showing off her new mobile phone to her friends. The phone was so tiny, you could hardly see it from here. It was the latest model, and nobody else in school had one yet. Even the teachers kept eyeing it jealously.

'*Amber!*'

'Oh, what is it now, Kim?' I asked irritably, without turning round. You know those people you are sort-of friends with because you can't be bothered to tell *them* not to bother? Kim and I are sort-of friends.

Chelsea and Sharelle think she's a waste of space.

'Help me!' Kim wailed, shooting past us. I hadn't realized she could run so fast. Her skinny little arms and legs were pumping away like pistons.

Hot on her heels was George Botley, who's in our class.

'What's going on?' I asked.

'I think Botley is threatening to put a worm down Kim's back,' Sharelle replied.

'Oh, right,' I said. 'So what about Botley? Looks, zero out of ten, obviously.'

'Style, minus ten,' Chelsea scoffed. 'Botley thinks style is turning his shirt collar up.'

We watched George chase Kim over to the other side of the playground. Kim was shrieking hysterically and not looking where she was going. She ploughed right through a group of Year 7 girls who were standing around chatting, scattering them right and left. From a distance, we could see the girls jumping up and down and shouting at her. One of them, my sister Jazz, stuck her foot out and sent George Botley rolling across the playground like a stuntman.

There are good and bad things about having sisters who are close to you in age. Geena's nearly fourteen, I'm twelve and Jazz is eleven. Geena always says that Mum and Dad liked her so much, they decided to have lots of babies close together, then they had me and Jazz and that was the start of the nightmare. It might have been funny once, a very long time ago.

At least we can borrow each other's clothes, even if we're different shapes and sizes. Geena's small and curvy with the kind of figure that makes boys walk into lampposts. I'm taller and skinnier, and Jazz is a mixture of the two. The three of us have dark hair and dark eyes, and in a strange way we all look like each other, and yet we don't. As if an incompetent Dr Frankenstein tried to make three clones of one person, and didn't quite succeed.

But, obviously, it's a total disadvantage to be so close in age when you're trying to win an argument. Sharelle's seven-year-old brother, for instance, has no chance against her. One arm lock, and it's all over before it's begun. On the other hand, our fights are often like the Hundred Years War. Long and bloody.

George was picking himself up and dusting himself down. I thought he might have a go at Jazz, but he didn't, because she started fluttering her eyelashes at him. Jazz flirts like she breathes, meaning all the time.

Kim was trying to hide behind the school flagpole, which was useless because bits of her were sticking out on either side. George spotted her immediately, and the chase was on again.

'Do you reckon Botley fancies Kim?' Chelsea asked.

'He's got a funny way of showing it,' I replied.

Sharelle grinned an evil grin. 'He fancies Amber. I've seen him staring at her in maths lessons.'

'He was just trying to copy my answers,' I said.

4

'Amber, did you see where Kim went?' Jazz was coming towards me, and she looked concerned. My sisters and I have this unspoken rule that we keep an eye on Kim because she's so totally useless. Brutal, but true. 'She's gone round the back of the school.'

The back of the lower school was out of bounds. The headmaster, Mr Morgan, who hardly ever bothered to pop across the road from his plush new office, had sent a message to tell us so. There were builders working round there, trying to prop the school up so that it would last another few months before we all moved to the new site. It was quite likely that Kim would faint with sheer terror once she realized that she'd broken a school rule, so I thought it was time I intervened.

I sneaked round to the back of the school, while the dinner ladies weren't looking. Jazz, Chelsea, Sharelle and some of the others followed me to see what was going on. So did Geena and her mates. There were a few Year 9 boys having a sneaky ciggie round there, and they slunk off, trying not to cough. George was there too, grinning all over his face, but there was no sign of Kim.

'Where is she?' I asked sternly.

'Up there,' George chuckled.

I looked skywards. The builders had left a very tall ladder propped against the wall, and Kim was clinging to the top of it, like a monkey to a tree.

'Kim!' I called, shading my eyes. 'Come down,

you idiot. And quick, before you get caught.'

Kim opened and closed her mouth, but no words were coming out.

'Don't worry about Botley,' I added. 'He's not going to touch you.'

'Says who?' George demanded.

'I do.'

I gave George a shove, and he looked remarkably pleased. I was afraid that he did fancy me, which was a frightening thought. Meanwhile, more and more people were drifting round the corner of the building towards us. We were drawing a crowd.

'Kim, I promise you that George is not going to put a worm down your back,' I said firmly.

'Thanks, Amber,' Kim wailed, staring down at me. 'But now I'm stuck.'

Everyone cheered.

'Kim, you are *not* stuck,' I said. 'All you've got to do is come down the way you went up.'

'I can't.' Kim's face was white as chalk. 'I'm scared of heights.'

'Fear of heights, that's called agoraphobia, isn't it?' Sharelle asked.

'No, that's fear of open spaces,' Geena replied authoritatively. 'Fear of heights is acrophobia.' She learned a whole list of phobias once, and then went round telling people that melissophobia was fear of bees, and peladophobia was fear of bald people. Jazz and I weren't sure if she'd made them up or not.

'Kim's got botleyphobia,' George chortled, quite wittily for him. 'That's fear of George.'

'George, shut up *now*,' I warned. 'Kim, don't think about it. Just come down.'

Kim hung on even tighter, her skirt billowing in the breeze. 'Can you see my knickers?' she called anxiously.

'No,' I lied.

'Yes, we can,' George said. 'They're pink with white flowers.'

The boys cheered. Kim's lip quivered. It was all getting out of hand.

'Kim, listen to me.' I tried not to sound annoyed. 'We'll all get into big trouble if we're caught here.'

Kim was swaying slightly from side to side. 'Amber, I'm having a panic attack,' she yelped. 'I can't breathe.'

'Come on, Kim, we practised this before,' I reminded her. 'Take a big breath. Now, breathe out slowly.'

Geena nudged me. 'We'd better do something, Amber.'

'Here come the dinner ladies,' Jazz added, as a posse of them rounded the corner and stood staring at us.

'Well, they're not going to be any use,' I said. 'What do you think we should do?' Jazz, Geena and I went into a sisterly huddle. Everyone else watched and waited.

'Maybe one of us should go up and get her,' Geena suggested. 'Before the dinner ladies start to panic.'

The dinner ladies were panicking already. They were unable to decide what to do, and trying to hide behind each other. Finally, Mrs Hubble, who was the bravest, shuffled forward.

'Now, Kim,' she said in a quavering voice, 'you come down from there this minute. And the rest of you, get back into the playground. You know you're not allowed round here.'

Kim's the only person in the school who's scared of Mrs Hubble, but still she didn't move. Neither did anyone else. Then the bell rang.

'There's the bell,' Mrs Hubble added hopelessly. 'Off you all go.'

Of course, everyone ignored her. They weren't going to miss a minute of this gripping drama. Instead, they all looked at me, Geena and Jazz. They were expecting us to sort this out.

Why? Because they think we're cool.

And you know what?

We are.

Dead cool.

'I'm coming to get you, Kim,' I said. 'Just hold on tight.'

I climbed onto the lower rungs of the ladder. Meanwhile, Geena and Jazz cleared away the boys who were hanging around trying to look up Kim's skirt.

They moved them on briskly, like policemen at a traffic accident.

'What's going on?' Mr Grimwade, head of the lower school, roared, exploding out of the building like a ball from a cannon. 'Oh, I must be dreaming, I thought the bell rang, but it can't have done, because look! All the kids are still outside.' He swept everyone with a ferocious glare. 'And you're all out of bounds. Will the detention room be big enough? I ask myself. Are the lower school going for the world record in detentions?'

'Kim's stuck up the ladder, sir,' Geena explained. 'Amber's gone to help her down.'

Mr Grimwade glanced up. 'Amber!' he bellowed. 'Hold it right there!'

I stopped halfway up the ladder. 'It's all right, sir,' I assured him. 'Everything's fine.'

'Yes, well, there is *no way* you should be up there,' Mr Grimwade blustered, looking pale. He was probably calculating the amount the school would have to pay in damages if Kim or I fell.

'I had to, sir,' I said simply. 'Kim was panicking.'

'I still am,' Kim gasped.

'Hm.' Mr Grimwade frowned. 'Well, it's a pity someone in authority didn't have the same initiative.'

He eyeballed the dinner ladies accusingly. They all shuffled their feet and looked sheepish.

'I've got varicose veins,' Mrs Hubble said tremulously.

'And what's Kim doing up there, anyway?' Mr Grimwade blustered on.

No one said anything, but they all turned to stare meaningfully at George Botley.

'Aha!' Grimwade said triumphantly. 'Botley, I'll speak to you later.'

A whole crowd of teachers sauntered out of school at that moment, carrying cups of coffee. They were trying to look concerned, but you could tell they were thrilled to have an extra few minutes' break.

'What's going on?' asked Mr Arora, my form tutor. Sleeping Beauty, we call him. Her name was Aurora. *Arora*, get it now? And it fits because he's pretty fine, too. Nearly all the girls in the school are in love with him.

'Kim's stuck up the ladder, sir, and Amber's gone to get her,' Jazz said.

'Good Lord, Amber,' Mr Arora said anxiously. He brushed his silky black hair gracefully out of his eyes, and half the lower school girls nearly fainted. 'I really don't think you should be doing that.'

'Kimberley Henderson!' yelled Miss Thomas, the head of girls' games who thought we were all wimps. 'Come down from there immediately!'

Kim turned even whiter and closed her eyes.

'She got stuck at the top of the rope ladder in the gym once,' Miss Thomas went on. 'I had to climb up and get her down myself. Stiff as a board, she was.'

'She's obviously got a fear of heights,' said Mrs

Kirke (environmental studies) sympathetically.

'What's that called?' Mr Arora asked, 'Agoraphobia?'

'No, sir, that's fear of open spaces,' chorused the watching crowd.

I left them to it and carried on climbing.

'Amber!' Mr Grimwade suddenly roared, and I nearly fell off the ladder. 'Be careful,' he added.

'I'm all right, sir.' I hoped Kim wasn't peladophobic, because the sun was glinting off Mr Grimwade's bald head and it was quite dazzling.

I was near the top of the ladder now, and Kim was looking down at me with big, frightened eyes. I stopped just behind her, and held out my hand. 'Come on. I'll help you.'

'But then I'll have to let go,' Kim said.

'Well, if you can think of any other way of getting down, let me know.'

We hung on there for a few minutes. Then George Botley's voice drifted up to us.

'This is just like one of those movies where the cops try to persuade someone not to jump off a building.'

'Have several detentions, George,' we heard Mr Grimwade offer.

'Come on, Kim.' I gave her ankle a gentle tug. 'I won't let you fall.'

'I *can't*,' Kim wailed.

Everyone was watching, faces upturned, waiting for me to succeed. Geena and Jazz were looking calm,

11

but I knew they were secretly anxious. I just could not afford to fail. We were winners, not losers.

'Kim,' I said quietly, so that no one else could hear. 'If you don't come down with me right now, I'm going to pull your skirt down and show *everyone* your knickers.'

'I'm on my way,' Kim said, feeling for the next rung down with her foot.

Everyone started cheering again, as we slowly climbed to safety. I jumped down from a few rungs up, and landed lightly on my feet like a cat. Everyone looked at me admiringly. Then Kim reached the bottom and collapsed into Geena's and Jazz's arms.

'Those builders are totally irresponsible,' Mr Grimwade grumbled under his breath. 'This area should be cordoned off. If anyone hurts themselves on this equipment, their parents will sue us to kingdom come.'

'True,' Mr Arora said in his heart-throb voice. 'We don't want one of the kids getting badly injured.'

'Yes, that as well,' Mr Grimwade agreed hastily. 'We'll have to make sure the building work's finished before . . .'

He didn't complete the sentence, but the teachers turned white. Everyone knew what he meant. The school inspectors were visiting Coppergate in just under three weeks' time, and nerves were jangling.

Geena and I put our arms round Kim, who could hardly walk because her knees were knocking together. Jazz picked up Kim's jacket, which she'd dropped at the bottom of the ladder. Everyone stood aside, even the teachers, as we led Kim into school. Only we could get away with breaking the school rules and become heroines.

'I don't know what we'd do without those girls,' said Mrs Kirke approvingly, before we were out of earshot.

Everyone loves us. The teachers like us because we work hard, and we're clever, polite and helpful. The other kids like us because we're pretty and popular and funny and smart. They even have a name for us. The Bindi Babes. No one's got more designer labels than we have. We've got everything we could ever want. Almost everything.

Remember what I said before? If people envy you, they're not pitying you. If people envy you, they're not looking at you and remembering what happened to your mum.

Our mum died.

It happens.

'I'm going to be in real trouble now,' Kim said weakly.

We were nearly at our classroom, but it was hard going. Geena and I were almost carrying Kim, who was sagging like a soft toy losing its stuffing.

'No, you won't,' I assured her. 'Anyway, just blame Botley.'

'Isn't that telling tales?' Kim asked doubtfully.

I shrugged. 'He's got hundreds of detentions this week already, so a few more won't make much difference.'

'I think I need the loo,' she mumbled, crossing her legs.

'Well, you're on your own then,' I said, and dropped her arm.

We waited till Kim had staggered into the girls' cloakroom before saying anything.

'So how did you get her down?' Geena asked.

'I said I'd show everyone her knickers,' I replied.

'Nice one,' Jazz said. 'Poor old Kim.'

We grinned at each other. Kim was scared of everything. For her, life was a big, ongoing problem. The three of us, on the other hand, weren't scared of anything at all. Life was pretty good, despite what it had thrown at us.

'Now, has anyone got anything to ask Dad tonight?' Geena asked in a businesslike way.

School was over, and we were on our way home. Kim was still feeling a bit wobbly, so we'd taken her to the tower block where she lives with her mum and Gary, her mum's boyfriend. In a flat, I mean. They don't own the whole block, ha ha.

'My ears,' Jazz began, and Geena and I groaned.

'Not again,' I said. 'I happen to think my new trainers are more important.'

'Why?' Jazz demanded aggressively.

'Because I've already told Chelsea and Sharelle that I'm getting them,' I replied.

'That was a bit risky,' Geena remarked. 'Seeing as you haven't even asked Dad yet.'

'Like he's really going to say no,' I scoffed. We tried not to ask Dad for too many things all at once, so we had regular discussions on the way home from school to plan our strategy. But it had been a month since I'd got the money for my DKNY sunglasses, so I reckoned my new trainers were as good as on my feet already.

'Anyway, Jazz, there's no point in asking Dad if you can get your ears pierced again,' I went on. 'He'll just say you have to wait till you're twelve, like he always does.'

'No, he won't.' Jazz gave me a shove. 'He's weakening. I can see it. He can't look me straight in the eye any more.'

'I want my bedroom redecorated,' Geena joined in. 'I saw a gorgeous purple and silver colour scheme on *Changing Rooms* last week.'

'You just fancy that bloke with the long hair,' I said.

'No, I do not,' Geena retorted, and we spent five minutes hitting each other with our bags.

'Geena, will you go out with my mate?' yelped a spotty Year 10 boy, who'd been following us for the last fifteen minutes.

'No, thank you,' Geena replied politely.

We get asked out all the time. Dad's quite strict and

he doesn't let us date boys. But we'll get round him when we feel like it.

'How about this for a brilliant word?' I announced, clipping Jazz lightly on the ear. '*Discombobulate.*'

'There's no such thing,' Geena accused me.

'Yes, there is.' I smiled. 'Now you've got to guess what it means.'

I didn't know what it meant myself, but it sounded great.

'You've discombobulated my head,' Jazz suggested, rubbing her ear.

'That dog's discombobulating,' Geena added, as an Alsatian cocked his leg against a lamppost.

'Nope.' I'd let them guess for a while, and then I'd make something up.

'Oh *no*,' Geena groaned. She was looking further down the street. 'That's all we need.'

There was Mr Attwal, standing in the doorway of his minimarket, searching for likely victims to bore to death.

I assessed the situation. 'We haven't got time to hide.'

'No, we haven't,' Geena said under her breath. 'Just stay cool, and remember: stick together.'

We stood shoulder to shoulder. It could be dangerous if one of us got left behind or separated. Bravely we marched along the pavement, looking straight ahead. If you accidentally made eye contact, it could be disastrous.

'Hello, girls,' Mr Attwal was already beginning hopefully, as we got closer. 'Not coming in today?'

'No, we're in a hurry,' Geena said brightly, still walking, still looking straight ahead.

'Not even for free sweets?' Mr Attwal offered.

We'd fallen for that one a couple of times before. Luckily, we were saved when a young mum with a baby in her arms crossed the road and walked towards the shop.

'Come in, madam.' Mr Attwal beamed. 'Welcome to my shop.' He handed the woman a wire basket, stepped aside, waved her in and patted the baby's head without drawing breath. 'Of course, I never expected to end up as a shopkeeper. I could have been an accountant, you know. Or a lawyer. My teachers in Delhi actually thought I'd make a very fine doctor . . .'

The mum and her baby were trapped, like flies in a spider's web. Meanwhile, the three of us rushed past gratefully.

'Personally, I think I could have been a computer wizard.' Mr Attwal's voice drifted after us. 'Of course, I've never used a computer. I just have this feeling . . .'

'He told me once that he could have been an astronaut,' Jazz whispered. 'He said he wanted to be the first man in orbit with a turban under his space helmet.'

'Do you remember—' I began, then stopped. About

17

five years ago, Mum had sent me to the corner shop for a loaf of bread. When I hadn't come home after an hour, she'd panicked, but it turned out I'd fallen asleep behind the fruit and veg while Mr Attwal was still talking, and he hadn't noticed. It was a family joke, but it meant mentioning Mum. And we never did.

The other two were looking at me, waiting for me to finish the sentence. Luckily, I spotted something to distract them.

'Isn't that Dad's car?'

'What? It *can't* be.' Geena shaded her eyes and looked down our street.

'It *is* Dad's car,' Jazz said. 'What's he doing here?'

That ought to have given us a clue. Dad was never home when we got back from school. We used to have a childminder called Mrs O'Connor, but about a month ago we'd persuaded Dad that we were old enough to look after ourselves until he got home from work. Dad was the head accountant with a big company, and he always seemed to have too much work to do. Half the time he didn't get back till ten or eleven at night, so we got takeaways and watched unsuitable TV programmes whenever we wanted. It was *great*.

'When was the last time Dad came home early from work?' Geena asked.

I thought about it. 'When Jazz fell over and split her head open,' I said. 'And Mrs O'Connor panicked.'

Jazz sniffed. 'She was more worried about missing *Neighbours* than about my poor head.'

'Well, it *was* just coming up to an exciting bit,' Geena said.

We hurried towards the house. Our next-door neighbour, Mrs Macey, was weeding her front garden and, as usual, she turned her back on us. She moved in six months ago, and she never speaks. We can't figure out if she doesn't like us because we're Indian, or because we're children. Maybe it's both. Or maybe she just doesn't like anyone. I've never seen her have any visitors.

'Mrs Macey's definitely discombobulated,' Geena said, unlocking the door with the key she kept on a chain round her neck.

'You know what?' I said. 'I reckon you're right.'

Dad came out of the living room as we burst through the door. He was wearing jeans and a denim shirt instead of a suit and tie, which was even more shocking. He'd come home and *changed*, which meant he wasn't going back to the office.

'What are you doing here, Dad?' Geena asked immediately. 'Is something wrong?'

Dad looked nervous, and that was enough to make my skin crawl with fear. It reminded me of coming home from school almost two years ago, and Dad telling us Mum was ill, and wasn't going to get well again. The memory was so strong, so bitter, I could almost taste it. I did what I always did, and pushed it right out of my mind, like a bad dream that had nothing to do with me, or my life.

'Nothing's wrong,' Dad replied, just as quickly. He took off his silver-rimmed glasses and polished them on his sleeve, while trying to look casual. That made me even more nervous. Dad always cleans his glasses when he's worried so he doesn't have to look us straight in the eye. 'I felt like finishing work early today.'

'Why?' Jazz said, opening her mouth just to put her foot in it.

Dad looked as awkward as we felt. 'Do I need a reason to come home to see my daughters?'

This was new ground, so we were a bit unsure how we should reply.

'No,' Geena said at last.

'Oh,' Jazz said.

'Great,' I added.

We stood and looked at each other.

'Well,' Dad said helplessly, replacing his glasses. 'What do you usually do at this time?'

'We make something to eat,' Geena offered.

'Something healthy and nourishing,' I added.

'Or we could get a takeaway from Perfect Pizza,' Jazz began. '*Ow!*'

She's such a drama queen. I'd only stamped on the very tip of her toes.

'Fine.' Dad looked relieved. 'Let's have something to eat then.'

We went into the kitchen, and Geena took two Marks and Spencer's lasagnes out of the freezer, while Dad laid the table. I made a salad, and Jazz sat on the worktop, swinging her legs.

'Why do you think Dad's come home early?' Geena asked, switching the microwave on. She looked worried.

'You heard what he said,' I replied, putting the boxes neatly into the bin. 'Maybe he's just come home to check up on us. You know he didn't really want to get rid of Mrs O'Connor.'

'That's true.' Geena cheered up. 'Jazz, you're sitting on a big blob of tomato ketchup.'

We sat down to eat. Dad was still looking nervous, which I couldn't understand. If he'd come home to check up on us, why would he look nervous? I glanced at Geena, who raised her eyebrows expressively at me. She was thinking the same thing. Jazz, as usual, was only thinking about herself.

'Dad, can I have my ears pierced again?' she demanded.

'What for?' Dad asked bravely. But Jazz was right, he was starting to cave. He was fidgeting in his chair and looking shifty. 'You've got two perfectly good holes already.'

'Geena and Amber have both got their ears pierced twice, *and* they've got their noses pierced as well,' Jazz whined. She's good at that.

'Yes, and we had to wait till we were twelve,'

Geena said. 'So you've got six months to go.'

'But I'm very mature for my age,' Jazz argued. 'I *feel* like I'm twelve already inside my head.'

'Well, I feel seventeen,' I said. 'Dad, can I have a car, please?'

Dad laughed, which delighted me. I liked making him laugh because it didn't happen very often these days. I didn't see him enough to do it regularly. But he soon shut up when Jazz stuck her bottom lip out and did a bit more whining.

'*Please*, Dad.'

'We'll see,' Dad said vaguely. He always looked a bit awkward and lost without Mum to back him up. The thought surfaced in my mind before I could stop it. Mum wouldn't have given in, whatever Jazz had said. *Don't think about it*, I reminded myself quickly.

Dad twirled his fork around, and I noticed he hadn't eaten anything. 'Listen for a minute,' he said. 'I need to talk to you.'

There's everyday kind of talking, and then there's *talking*. Dad and the three of us didn't *talk* since Mum. I wondered what he was going to say.

'Yes, well . . .' Dad fidgeted about for a bit. 'We haven't had a very easy time of it for the last year or so, have we?'

We all looked down at our plates. He *couldn't* talk about Mum. We didn't, because that was the only way everything was bearable.

'So, I think it's time there were a few changes around here,' Dad went on.

'Changes?' I repeated suspiciously. 'What kind of changes?'

I could tell that Geena and Jazz were thinking exactly the same as I was. Why did we need changes? Everything was as good as it could be, under the circumstances.

Dad cleared his throat. 'You remember your aunt in India,' he said hopefully.

Aunt?

'What aunt?' Jazz asked, opening her eyes wide. 'We haven't got an aunt in India.'

'Yes, we have, no-brain,' I said across the table.

'Oh, *that* aunt,' Jazz said. 'The one who doesn't like us.'

'Oh, Jazz, *really*.' Dad looked nervous. 'That's not true.'

It was. She was my dad's sister, but we didn't know her at all. She'd visited us in England once, years ago, but she and our mum didn't get on, so she'd never come back.

'Auntie's very fond of you,' Dad went on.

We didn't say anything. I couldn't even remember what Auntie looked like. I was five the last time I saw her.

'Auntie's coming over from India to live with us,' Dad said. 'She's going to look after us. Won't that be nice?' He stared intently at his plate.

'*What?*' Geena said.

'When?' I demanded.

'Now I'm *really* discombobulated,' Jazz announced sulkily.

There was no answer to that.

CHAPTER 2

We didn't want her, of course. Why would we? We had everything going for us. Dad gave us anything we wanted, eventually. Everyone at school thought we were the best. The teachers loved us. Nearly all the boys fancied us. We could do pretty much what we liked as long as we behaved ourselves and did our homework on time. Life was good.

Of course we didn't want her. We didn't *need* her.

'I can't believe Dad would do this to us,' Geena said for the seventh or eighth time. It was the following morning. Dad had escaped to the office before we got up, so there was no chance to have another go at him. 'This is going to ruin *everything*.'

'So what are we going to do about it?' I asked. 'Jazz, if you've nicked my only clean shirt, I'm going to kill you very slowly.'

'I haven't,' Jazz retorted, putting her school sweatshirt on quickly.

'It *looks* like mine.'

'They're all exactly the same,' Jazz said smugly.

'They're uniform. That's what it means. Uniform means all the same— Urgh!'

I'd grabbed her round the neck. 'Give me that shirt.'

'Geena, help me!' Jazz croaked, as I tightened my grip.

'Oh, for God's sake.' Geena took a clean shirt out of her wardrobe, and handed it to me. 'We've got more important things to talk about.'

She was right. Jazz and I slapped each other around a bit, and then declared a truce.

'Maybe we can stop Auntie from coming,' Jazz suggested, as we clattered downstairs.

'How?' I asked. 'Hijack the plane?'

'We could ring the Foreign Office, and tell them she's an international criminal,' Jazz said. 'We could say she's smuggling drugs under her sari.'

'Pity she isn't married,' I grumbled. 'If she had her own family to look after, then she wouldn't have to come and interfere with ours.'

'I heard Mum say once that nobody would be daft enough to marry her,' Geena blurted out. Then she stopped, looking horrified. Jazz and I immediately leaped in to cover for her.

'How old is Auntie anyway?' Jazz asked.

And at exactly the same moment, I said, 'Didn't she have to look after Biji and Babaji?' Our grandparents had been quite old when they'd married and had Dad and Auntie, and they'd died only six months apart two years ago. They'd never come to England and I'd only seen them once, when Mum and Dad had taken Geena, me and baby Jazz to India years ago. My memories of Biji and Babaji were even more hazy than my memories of Auntie.

Geena cleared her throat, still looking a bit pale. 'She's a bit younger than Dad,' she mumbled. 'About thirty?'

'She's getting old,' Jazz remarked severely. 'No one'll *want* to marry her if she doesn't get a move on.'

'When did Dad say she was arriving?' Geena asked.

'He didn't,' I replied. 'He just said sometime soon.'

'That's a bit suspicious, don't you think?' Geena said thoughtfully. 'Maybe they're trying to take us by surprise.'

'We've got to make sure we're ready for her, whatever happens,' I said.

It all made sense now. Why Dad had agreed to get rid of Mrs O'Connor last month. He must have known for weeks that Auntie was coming, but he hadn't said a word.

One thing was certain. Auntie might *think* she was coming to take our mum's place. But we knew better.

We ate breakfast and got ready to leave. We loaded the dishwasher and wiped the worktops and emptied the kitchen bin. Did we need anybody to look after us? No, we didn't. We were doing a fine job on our own.

'You know what's going to happen, don't you?' I predicted, as we left the house. '*She's* going to interfere in *everything*.' I banged the door shut behind us. 'No more takeaways. No more late-night TV. No more—'

I turned and got a *Daily Telegraph* smack in the face.

'You scumbag!' I charged down the path after the paperboy. Meanwhile, Geena and Jazz laughed their heads off. 'You are so dead!'

The paperboy stuck two fingers up at me, stopped at Mrs Macey's gate, hurled the *Sun* into her porch and cycled off. I glared after him.

'Why can't you open the gate, walk up the path and put the newspaper through the letter box like a normal person?' I hollered.

I was really angry, though it was hard to explain why. It was more than the useless paperboy chucking a *Daily Telegraph* at me. Here we were, trying our best to get on with things and cope with all that had happened. And there everyone else was, trying to make life really difficult for us. 'Everyone else' included Dad.

'Anything good in the paper, Amber?' Geena asked me with a grin.

'Ha ha.' I stuffed the *Telegraph* savagely through our letter box. 'So what *are* we going to do about Auntie? Any ideas?'

We decided to walk, rather than get the school bus, so that we could discuss our anti-Auntie campaign in peace. The bus was always noisy, and the driver would be threatening to throw everyone off and leave us stranded in the High Street if we didn't behave ourselves. Or worse, he would be muttering about ways of killing us all, slowly and horribly. And boys would be pestering us for dates. Or they'd annoy us by flicking bits of paper or kicking our seats, and pretending they *didn't* fancy us. We weren't in the mood.

'Morning, girls.' Mr Attwal was unlocking the minimarket. 'I hear your auntie's coming to live with you.'

So he knew as well. That meant everyone else for miles around knew. You can't keep anything quiet round here. If you sneeze, everyone discusses it.

'How do *you* know?' Jazz asked.

'Your dad told Mr Dhaliwal yesterday, and he told Mr Chopra and he told me.' Mr Attwal frowned. 'Or was it Manjit from number twelve?'

'Did he say *when* she was coming?' I asked.

Mr Attwal shook his head. 'Can't wait, eh, Amber?' he smiled.

'That's right,' I said bitterly.

'You must really be looking forward to it,' Mr Attwal went on. I don't know where he got that idea from. Did we look pleased? 'What does she do?'

'She teaches English in a girls' school,' Geena replied.

Oops.

29

'Ah, a teacher.' Mr Attwal's eyes took on a faraway look. 'Many years ago, when I was at school in Delhi—'

'Got to go or we'll be late for school,' we gabbled, and fled.

'Sorry, guys.' Geena was kicking herself. 'He caught me off-guard.'

I glanced at my watch. 'Let's get a move on. It's quarter past eight.'

There was no way we could be late. We were never late for school, or anywhere. How could we show how well we were coping, unless we were perfect in almost every way?

'About Auntie,' Geena said as we speeded up. 'What are we going to do?'

'Well, show her she's not wanted, for a start,' I said. 'I mean, we do our own cooking, cleaning, washing—'

'It might be nice to have someone else do it,' Jazz offered. Then backtracked quickly when she saw our faces. 'Not Auntie, though.'

'Amber!'

Kim was scuttling down the street towards us. As usual, she was carrying her over-stuffed rucksack, which bent her in two and made her look like a giant tortoise.

'I thought we were getting the bus this morning,' she panted.

'Sorry.' I'd forgotten about Kim. I did that quite a

lot, without meaning to. 'We've got problems.'

'Oh.' Kim's face was always pale, but today she looked totally colourless. 'Me too.'

I tried not to look irritated. Kim's always got problems. She has a panic attack if she loses her pencil case.

'No, *real* problems,' I said. Kim's face fell, but I ignored her. 'Our auntie's coming over from India to live with us.'

We all looked expectantly at Kim.

'And?' Kim said, looking expectantly back at *us*.

'That's it,' I said.

'That's it?' Kim looked puzzled. Then she saw my face and finally got it. 'Oh. That's terrible. Really, really terrible.'

I sometimes wonder why I'm friends with Kim. She started hanging around with me in the Infants because I stopped George Botley from painting her face blue once, and she's hung around ever since. A bit like a piece of chewing gum stuck to your shoe.

'Yes, it is,' I said. 'She's going to interfere and boss us around. Like we're *really* going to put up with it.'

'Is she awful?' Kim asked.

Jazz and I looked at Geena. She was the only one of us who could possibly remember anything about Auntie's visit all those years ago.

'Hmm.' Geena wrinkled up her nose. 'She's sort of . . . *pretty*.'

'*Pretty?*' Jazz and I shrieked. If Geena had said

Auntie was a serial killer, we couldn't have been more shocked.

'Wow,' said Kim. 'That sounds bad.'

I looked at her suspiciously, but let it go. Kim doesn't usually do sarcasm.

'Sorry,' Geena apologized. 'That's all I can remember.'

It wasn't really much to go on.

'I bet she's like Modern Auntie in *Goodness Gracious Me,*' I said. 'She'll have too much make-up on, and she'll keep hugging us all the time.'

'Or pinch our cheeks,' Jazz added. Cheek-pinching is something our relatives love to do. It's embarrassing. Painful, too.

'She'll be really strict and she won't let us go anywhere or do anything,' Geena grumbled. Dad was strict too, but he was never there so that was all right.

We walked towards the lower school playground. Someone had written I LOVE GEENA in blue chalk on the wall, and underneath, in yellow, was written I LOVE AMBER. To the side of that, someone had drawn a big pink heart, and chalked JAZZ 4 EVER inside it. There were some much ruder comments about us as well, but we hardly took any notice. We were used to the attention, good and bad, and we weren't stupid enough to think that everybody liked us. Two years ago, Geena had smacked a girl who called me a Paki on my first day.

'I've got another present for you, Kim.' George Botley was on the watch for us, grinning all over his face. 'Come and get it.'

He held out his hand, which was curled tightly shut.

'Keep away from me, Botley,' Kim sniffed, trying not to look petrified.

'Oh, go on.' George winked. 'You know you want to.'

He unfurled his fingers. A large, fat snail sat wetly on his palm.

'You pig, George Botley!' Kim howled, running behind me.

'Give me that.' I took the snail, which retreated into its shell, and put it down carefully on the grass. 'What a slimy, nasty, horrible thing.'

'Snails aren't horrible,' George protested.

'Who said I was talking about the snail?' I said, eyeballing him. George roared with laughter and sauntered off.

'He fancies you,' Kim said gloomily. 'That's why he keeps picking on me.'

'Maybe he fancies *you*,' I pointed out.

'Nobody fancies me,' Kim muttered. Once she starts her 'poor me' routine, there's no stopping her. The only solution is to ignore her.

'So what *are* we going to do about Auntie?' Jazz asked impatiently.

'I don't know yet,' Geena said. 'We need to think

about it. We need to discuss it. We can't make our minds up just like that.'

'In other words, you don't know,' I said.

'That's right,' Geena agreed. 'But we'll think of something.'

'The important thing is not to *worry* about it,' Mr Grimwade boomed, glaring round the lower school assembly hall. 'The inspectors are simply coming here to *help* and *advise* us. The headmaster has asked me to reassure you again that there's nothing to be afraid of at all.'

We were getting our weekly pep talk about the inspectors visiting Coppergate. Despite his brave words, Mr Grimwade never fooled anyone. The pupils didn't look worried at all, though. It was the teachers who were as white as ghosts.

'As you can see, the teachers aren't worrying at all,' Grimwade went on, baring his teeth, the closest he ever got to a smile. 'They're very relaxed about it.'

Mrs Murray, who was at the piano, twitched nervously and knocked over a music stand. It crashed heavily down on a member of the orchestra sitting next to her.

'There's nothing *at all* to worry about,' repeated Mr Grimwade savagely, as the injured recorder player was helped from the hall. 'But we *do* expect every one of you to be on your best behaviour when the inspectors arrive.'

'Here we go again,' muttered George Botley, who was sitting two down from me, Chelsea and Sharelle. 'What's in it for us?'

'There are some of you who are certainly a credit to the school.' Mr Grimwade's gaze targeted Jazz, who was sitting with Year 7 several rows in front of me. His eyes met mine briefly, and then moved to the back of the hall. I didn't need to look round to know he had singled out Geena. 'But there are some of you who really need to pull your socks up and do a whole lot better.'

He eyed George Botley belligerently.

'Remember, we are all part of the great community which is Coppergate School, and I'm sure everyone wants to impress the inspectors with our hard work, dedication, good manners and our school spirit.' Mr Grimwade leaned forward, sweeping the hall with a single glare. 'Know now that I shall personally make it my mission in life to seek out and destroy anyone who steps out of line while the inspectors are here. That is all.'

We stood up. The Year 7 classes went out first, from the front. I noticed Jazz was flanked by two boys, one on either side of her like bodyguards. They were both smiling proudly. They'd probably had to bribe or fight the other boys in the class to get to stand next to her.

'Off you go, Eight D,' said Miss Thomas, whose class was next to leave. As always, I said a silent prayer of thanks that Mr Arora was our form teacher, and not Thomas the Tank Engine.

'No, no, *no*!' Miss Thomas hissed, as 8D began shambling out of the hall. She rolled her eyes. 'Like we practised *yesterday*. Lead with the right foot, and keep in time. March, Eight D, *march*.'

'Thomas is going all out to impress the inspectors,' Sharelle whispered in my ear, while the rest of the school waited patiently for their turn to leave.

Cursing sulkily under their breath, 8D tried to get into step. They failed spectacularly.

'Right!' Miss Thomas snapped, 'Back up, Eight D, and start again.'

'I think we'd better go, Eight A,' Mr Arora said mildly. 'It looks like Eight D might be some time.'

'Amber, a word with you, please.' Mr Arora caught up with me in the corridor, as we went back to class.

'Yes, sir?' I put my speaking-to-teachers mask on. It was smiling and helpful, but cool and slightly reserved at the same time, so the other kids didn't think I was a creep. It took a lot of doing, but I was an expert by now.

'Ms Woods wants to see you sometime today.' Mr Arora smiled at me, and half the girls in the corridor sighed longingly. It created a noticeable breeze. 'She's planning a special assembly for the day the inspectors arrive, and she'd like you to be involved.'

'Doing what, sir?' I asked. Ms Woods was the head

of drama. I'd been a favourite of hers ever since I'd played Aladdin in the lower-school panto last year. George Botley had hidden a stink bomb inside Aladdin's magic lamp, but I'd found it in time and lobbed it out of the window like a member of the SAS. Ms Woods had been very impressed.

'She's not sure yet.' Mr Arora frowned, which, strangely, only made him look more gorgeous. 'But both the lower and upper schools will be taking part, so it will be held in the big new hall. Ms Woods is thinking along the lines of a pageant about the history of the school. Or maybe a musical introduction to some of the world's great religions. Something like that.'

'Just a normal Monday morning assembly then,' was what I wanted to say, very sarcastically. But I didn't. If Ms Woods wanted a West End extravaganza of singing and dancing to greet the inspectors when they arrived, it wasn't up to me to complain. After all, I'd probably have a starring part. So, very likely, would Geena and Jazz.

'As Mr Grimwade said,' Mr Arora went on, as we reached our classroom, 'we'll be expecting everyone to do their best when the inspectors are here. Some, of course, will do better than others.' He smiled gently at me, then switched it off like a light to glare at George Botley, who was making rude noises with his hand in his armpit. 'Let's just say that we'll be relying on those people to show Coppergate in its best possible light.'

'Yes, sir.' I knew exactly what he meant. If the school was on show for the inspectors, Geena, Jazz and I would be expected to perform, and perform brilliantly. Like we always did.

'Did you get the big lecture, Amber?' Jazz asked. We were on our way home later that day.

I nodded. 'From every single teacher I've seen today. Mr Arora, Miss Patel, Mrs Kirke, Miss Gordon . . .'

'Me too,' Geena said.

'And me,' Jazz added.

'Are you in Ms Woods's assembly?' I asked.

Both Geena and Jazz nodded, as I knew they would.

'Is it true Ms Woods is hiring an orchestra?' Jazz asked.

'I heard it was a gospel choir,' Geena offered. 'And someone said the whole hall is going to be turned into a scale replica of St Paul's Cathedral.'

'It wouldn't surprise me,' I replied.

We turned the corner into our street. Geena was in front, and she suddenly did that thing of stopping dead, so that Jazz and I rammed right into the back of her.

'Oof!' Jazz complained, holding her nose. 'What did you do that for?'

'Is Dad home again today?' I asked, peering round Geena's back. 'Because if he is, there's a few things I want to say to him.'

'No, Dad's car's not there.' Geena pointed down

our street. 'Look. Look at the windows.'

Even from the corner, a couple of hundred metres away, we could see that our living-room windows were flung wide open. We could see the blue curtains fluttering in the breeze.

'What's going on?' Jazz asked, bewildered. 'Who's opened the windows?'

'Burglars?' Geena's eyes were huge and worried.

'Burglars who like fresh air, by the look of it,' I said.

I was trying to lighten everyone up, but Geena turned on me.

'Shut up, Amber. This is serious.'

'All right,' I snapped. 'Got any bright ideas?'

'We could stop at Mrs Macey's, and ask her if she saw anyone go in,' Jazz suggested.

'She won't open the door,' I replied. 'You know what she's like.'

'Let's walk past and have a look,' Geena said urgently.

We marched down the road and past our front gate, trying to look casual. As we went by, we sneaked a look through the open windows.

'The TV, video and DVD player are still there,' Geena said in a low voice. 'So is the CD player.'

We all marched back again, stood by the gate and peered in.

'Maybe the burglar's started in the bedrooms,' I said in a low voice. 'There's lots of . . . stuff up there.' I was thinking of Mum's gold jewellery, packed away with her silk and satin saris in suitcases and boxes which hadn't been opened for a year.

'Oh, this is ridiculous,' Geena said. 'I'm going to take a proper look. You two wait here,' she went on, coming over all big-sisterly. 'It might be dangerous.'

Jazz and I waited until Geena had tiptoed up the path. Then, of course, we followed her. We looked over her shoulder into the living room.

We couldn't see anyone, but someone had been there. All the things we would have done when we got home from school had already happened. The room had been tidied and the carpet had been hoovered and the surfaces had been polished.

We were mesmerized. The evening newspaper came flying over our heads and landed with a thud in the porch, but even that didn't make us turn round.

'I've got it,' I said. 'It's a burglar who breaks in, cleans your house and leaves.'

'Ssh.' Geena clutched our arms. 'Listen. There's someone in the kitchen.'

Someone was moving around at the back of the house. Without saying a word, the three of us crept over to the side gate. Geena unlatched it, and we all took a deep breath before going in.

The back door was propped open. A woman in a pink shalwar kameez, her long black hair pinned up in an untidy topknot, was standing at the oven. She was stirring a big pot with a wooden spoon. Onions were sizzling in a pan, and the scent of spices floated in the warm air. Masala, ginger, turmeric and coriander.

Time spun backwards. I remembered running home from primary school, one hand in Jazz's and one hand in Geena's, our long plaits flying. Mum would be in the kitchen, making curry. The scent of the spices was the same, and the sound of the onions cooking. They took me back to a time when everything was known and safe.

The picture splintered. Shattered. The sounds and the smells were the same, but it wasn't Mum. This woman was a stranger, although I knew who she was. Dad had ducked out of telling us that Auntie was already on her way. In fact, he'd waited till the last possible minute to tell us at all.

I felt sick. *She* had no right to be standing there, in my mum's place. And I knew that Geena and Jazz felt the same. If we'd been younger, we would probably have taken each other's hands. Instead we moved closer together and stood shoulder to shoulder.

Auntie turned round. She didn't look anything like Dad. Dad is tall and thin and has long, spidery arms and legs. She was short and curvy. But to my surprise, I did remember her face. It was round and smiley, with two dimples. She had big eyes, which were very dark and shiny. They immediately filled with tears.

'Geena, Ambajit.' Auntie tried to hug us all at once. 'Jasvinder.'

We stood there, stiff as boards with embarrassment and anger, while she sniffed and fished in her sleeve for a hankie.

'I was so sorry about your mum,' she said.

We stayed silent. I wouldn't have said anything then, not for a million pounds. But I was thinking, Why? You weren't even friends.

'I arrived this morning. Your dad picked me up and then went back to work.' She was answering all the questions we were supposed to be asking, but weren't. 'How are you all? You look well.'

How much longer could she keep talking without any of us replying?

'Are you hungry? Shall we eat?' Auntie was at last beginning to run down. 'The curry's nearly ready. We can have a good chat. I want to hear all about your school, and how you're getting on. We've got so much to catch up on.'

'We've got homework to do,' I said, politely but coldly.

Auntie's smile faded. She looked me up and down slowly and thoughtfully, then her gaze moved to Geena and Jazz. She would have had to be deaf, dumb and blind not to sense the hostility coming off us in waves. She didn't say anything, but I could read the sudden knowing expression on her face. *So that's the way it's going to be, is it?*

Yes, I replied silently. *So get used to it.*

CHAPTER 3

'Jazz, is that you?'

'Is what me?' Jazz was curled up on her side of the bed, reading a magazine.

'That smell.' I flapped the duvet irritably.

'No, it isn't me,' Jazz snapped.

'Well, it's around here somewhere.' I glared at her. 'Is that my copy of *Bliss*?'

Jazz didn't look up. 'No.'

'Let me see it then.' I lunged towards her.

'Get off!' Jazz squealed, whacking me round the head with the magazine. 'I hate sharing with you.'

'Well, I hate sharing with you too!' I yelled, shoving her hard. We hadn't shared a bed since we were tiny, and I'd forgotten how much Jazz fidgeted and grunted and kicked. Last night had been like sleeping with a bag of monkeys. Guess who'd got *my* room.

'Aargh!' Jazz rolled over, and fell half out of the bed. I pounced on her.

'Give me the magazine!'

'NO.' Jazz stuffed it down the front of her pyjamas,

43

which made me really mad. So I grabbed a big hand-ful of her hair and pulled. She screamed, quite loudly.

'Give. Me. That. Magazine,' I hissed, bouncing up and down on top of her. 'Or I'm going to pull all your hair out, bit by bit, and you'll be bald all over like Mr Grimwade—'

I stopped there. Auntie was standing in the doorway, hands on her hips.

'What's going on?' she asked.

'Nothing.' I jumped to my feet and slid my hand behind my back. It still had some of Jazz's hair attached to it.

'Jasvinder?' Auntie looked at Jazz.

'Nothing,' Jazz said sulkily, rubbing her scalp.

I stared back at Auntie and smiled very slightly. There was nothing she could do. We'd closed ranks.

'All right.' Auntie shrugged and turned away. 'Make sure you give Jazz her hair back, Amber,' she added as she went out.

'She thinks she's so great,' I muttered.

'Here's your stupid magazine.' Jazz pulled it out of her pyjama top, and threw it at me.

'It's cool.' I tossed it back to her. 'It's last month's anyway.'

Auntie had already started interfering. Last night, Dad had come home in time for dinner, looking very embarrassed. No surprise there. We'd been thrown right into this thing before we'd had a chance to come up with a decent plan of action. I hadn't even had a chance to talk to the others properly without Auntie hanging around, spying on us and asking if we'd done our homework.

Anyway, the best way had to be to start as we meant to go on. To show Auntie we didn't need her. Show her that she couldn't boss us around. Show her that Dad was on our side, not hers.

'Dad, when can I get my new trainers?' I'd asked as we sat eating dinner.

'New trainers?' Auntie chimed in, before Dad had a chance to open his mouth. She bent sideways and looked at my feet under the table. 'What are those things you've got on then? Wellington boots?'

'Ha ha,' I said, freezingly polite. 'These are my *old* trainers.'

Auntie stared me challengingly in the eye. 'They look new to me.'

'They're not new at all,' I said a shade too quickly. I'd had them for about three months. 'Anyway, I'm bored with them.' I didn't look at Auntie, but at Dad.

'That sounds like a waste of money,' Auntie said pleasantly but firmly. She looked at Dad too. 'I hope you're going to say no.'

I did a double take. I must have looked like some actress in a bad sitcom. What did it have to do with *her*?

Dad looked embarrassed and apologetic. 'Your auntie's right, Amber,' he muttered. 'You don't need new trainers at the moment.'

Geena and Jazz looked as stunned as I was. Dad hardly ever said no to anything. Not since Mum.

'More curry, anyone?' Auntie asked briskly.

The three of us made faces at each other and seethed in silence for a bit. I could tell that Geena had decided to keep quiet about getting her bedroom redecorated, for the moment. But then Jazz returned to the attack.

'Dad, can I have my ears pierced this weekend?'

'What do you mean?' Auntie peered at Jazz's ears. It was seriously beginning to wind me up, how we asked Dad questions and she answered. 'Your ears are already pierced.'

'I want two more holes,' Jazz explained.

'Why?' Auntie wanted to know. 'You've only got one pair of ears.'

Jazz stuck her nose in the air. 'I'm asking *Dad*,' she said.

'And your dad's saying no.' Auntie turned round to look enquiringly at Dad. 'Isn't he?'

'No,' Dad said helplessly. 'I mean, yes. Yes, I'm saying no.'

'That's not fair,' Jazz gasped.

Auntie shook her head. 'Life isn't fair, Jasvinder,' she said. 'Have another chapati.'

You can see what we were up against. After dinner, Geena, Jazz and I sat ourselves down in front of the TV, maintaining a frosty silence. Meanwhile, Dad and Auntie talked. They didn't say anything about what had happened over the last few years. Instead they talked about when they were kids growing up in the family village in the Punjab.

'Remember that bad-tempered bullock we were both really scared of?' Auntie said, laughing. 'I used to hate feeding it every day.'

Dad nodded. 'Remember when it escaped from the pen and got out into the sugar cane fields? It took us ages to catch it.'

They talked about playing cricket in the fields, riding on the back of their dad's motorbike, going to the nearest town to watch Bollywood films at the cinema, chewing sugar cane, milking the cows, sitting on the flat roof of the house listening to the peacocks calling to each other. I tried not to listen, but I couldn't help it. It was a long time since Dad had looked like he was enjoying himself.

And yet all the time they were talking, I could see that Dad felt just a little uncomfortable. Auntie's arrival had changed everything for *him*, too. Which ignited a faint spark of hope inside me. Maybe Dad didn't *really* want Auntie there either . . .

Jazz and I climbed back into bed, and snuggled down under the duvet. We often got up early and went into town on Saturday mornings, but today we'd decided to stay in bed. We thought it might annoy Auntie, which was what we were aiming for. There was a Bollywood film on BBC2 we wanted to watch, which went on for nearly three hours. Bollywood films are long. That meant we could avoid Auntie all morning.

'Oh, you're awake.' Geena came in, still wearing her CK nightshirt. 'Who was that I heard screaming a few minutes ago?'

'Auntie,' I said. 'We tied her up and locked her in the airing cupboard.'

'Best place for her.' Geena climbed under the duvet at the bottom of the bed, and squeezed herself between our feet. 'Can you *believe* what she did last night?'

'Ssh.' Jazz cocked her head to one side. 'I can hear something.'

Dad and Auntie were outside on the landing, talking. Arguing.

'You're not going into work today, are you, Johnny?' Auntie was complaining. 'Not when I've only just arrived?'

'Wrong,' I whispered. Dad always goes to work on Saturdays. He had done so ever since Mum. Sometimes Sundays too. He didn't seem to want to be in the house at all. Maybe it was because it reminded him of Mum. Maybe we reminded him too.

'And I'm sure the girls would like to spend some time with you,' Auntie went on. 'You don't seem to see much of them at all.'

'Leave us out of it,' Geena said in a low voice.

We couldn't hear what Dad was saying. But a few minutes later, we heard the front door close.

48

'Well, she didn't win *that* one,' I said gleefully.

'Put the telly on, Jazz,' Geena ordered. 'It's time for *Reena aur Meena*.'

'Why me?' Jazz moaned.

'Because it's your telly,' Geena said.

'Amber's nearest.'

'I've hurt my foot,' I replied.

'You haven't,' Jazz said.

I kicked her under the duvet. 'Ow. I have now.'

'Screamingly funny,' Jazz sniffed. She got out of bed, and switched the TV on. The credits were just starting, and *Reena aur Meena* filled the screen in big, yellow letters.

'Oh, great, Shakila Devi's in it,' I said. She's our favourite actress.

The door opened, and Auntie came in.

'Not dressed yet?' she asked, raising her eyebrows.

'We're watching *Reena aur Meena*,' Geena explained.

'You can video it, can't you?' Auntie said. 'I thought we might do something together this morning.'

We looked at each other in shock.

'We'd like to watch the film *now*, if you don't mind, Auntie,' Geena replied politely.

'I don't blame you, actually,' Auntie said chattily, folding her arms. 'It's a really good movie. Reena and Meena are identical twins, but they get separated at birth from their mum and dad. Reena gets adopted by some rich people, and Meena gets kidnapped by some bandits.'

We stared pointedly at her. The film was starting, and we couldn't hear a word.

'Then they grow up, and when Reena's on her way to marry the hero, she gets captured by the bandits,' Auntie went on, so enthusiastically I could have strangled her. 'And Meena goes to the wedding in her place. So then *Meena* gets married to the hero, while *Reena* has to become a bandit. And then— Oh, wait a minute, I've missed a bit—'

'I'll find a blank video,' Geena said quickly, jumping out from underneath the duvet.

'Oh, are you sure?' Auntie settled herself comfortably on the bed. 'We could always watch it together.'

'I'm sure,' Geena said, her face grim.

Auntie shrugged, and went out. I wasn't sure, but I *thought* I could hear her laughing to herself.

'What do you think she wants to do?' Jazz grumbled, throwing back the duvet.

'Probably go shopping or something,' I said. 'Why can't she just leave us alone?'

Geena came back with the videotape. 'I know how we could *really* freak her out,' she said, smiling wickedly.

It took us half an hour to get ready. Short skirts, tiny T-shirts, hair mascara, glittery eye shadow, shiny lip gloss, fake tattoos, nail transfers. Everything. We had quite a bit of stuff that Dad had never seen, and wouldn't have liked, which we kept for school discos.

By the time we'd finished, we looked fab. Far too glam for a visit to Tesco.

'She won't want to go shopping with us *now*,' I said with satisfaction.

If we did go out like this, we'd be the talk of our street, as well as several other streets round about. The Indian families always kept an eye on each other, and reported back to the parents if they thought the kids looked too outrageous. When Baljeet Baines from down the road dyed her hair blonde, everyone had gossiped about it for weeks. It was like being stalked by the anti-fashion police. Dad was all right. He let us wear mostly what we wanted. Sometimes it was stuff from New Look and Top Shop, sometimes it was suits from the sari shop. But a lot of the Indian parents we knew spent all their time trying to stop their daughters wearing fashionable clothes. On school disco days, some of the girls would sneak their cool clothes out of the house in carrier bags. Then they'd get dressed up in the girls' loos. It was all a bit sad, really.

Triumphantly we went downstairs. Geena nearly went head-over-heels in her patent leather boots with stiletto heels, but she said it was worth it to see Auntie's face.

Auntie was in the kitchen, frying pakoras. When she saw us, her eyebrows shot up and nearly disappeared off her head. We gave her a polite, but evil smile.

'Aren't you a bit overdressed for cooking?' Auntie asked. She lifted a pakora out of the boiling oil with a fish slice.

'*Cooking?*' we shrieked.

'Yes, cooking.' Auntie lifted out another pakora, and added it to the pile. 'I've had a look in the freezer and there's barely anything in there at all. Do you girls live on takeaways?'

'No, of course not,' I said, lying with ease.

'Auntie, isn't it a bit sexist to expect us to cook, just because we're girls?' Geena said politely through her teeth. 'There's more to life than making meals.'

Auntie raised her eyebrows. 'We can discuss football or cars while we're cooking, if that makes you feel any better,' she said, rather sarcastically. 'Or what about computers? I'm doing a correspondence course in computer maintenance at the moment. Or cricket. I love watching cricket. What do you think of India's chances in the Test match?'

That shut us up.

'One of you can chop the potatoes for the samosas, while the other two make the pastry,' she went on. 'Everything's laid out ready on the worktop.'

Auntie passed me a knife and handed Geena and Jazz a large bowl. Sullenly I began chopping the boiled potatoes, while Geena and Jazz sulkily added butter and jeera seeds to the flour. We were speechless with fury. What a waste of a Saturday morning.

'How's school?' Auntie asked.

'All right,' Geena muttered.

'Are you behaving yourselves?'

'Yes,' I said.

'And are you working hard?'

We let Jazz answer that. 'Yes.'

There was silence.

'I'm sure your mum would be very proud of you.'

My heart stumbled and missed a beat. *Shut up*, I thought. I mixed the diced potatoes savagely with the peas, and Geena and Jazz kept their heads down over the flour. Auntie sighed and turned back to the frying pan.

The large drum of chilli pepper on the worktop caught my eye. I put down my wooden spoon, reached for it and poured a huge stream of pepper into the bowl. Then I mixed it quickly into the potatoes and peas. Any visitors we had were in for a red-hot surprise. They wouldn't be coming back for more of Auntie's cooking in a hurry.

'That'll teach her,' I muttered.

'What did you say, Amber?' Auntie turned to me.

'Nothing.'

Geena, Jazz and I made eight samosas, while Auntie finished cooking the pakoras. I kept nodding and winking at Geena and Amber, but they didn't get it. Sisterly telepathy does not exist. I found that out when we'd tidied up, and Auntie looked at the clock.

'It's just about lunch time,' she said. 'We'll have some of the samosas.' She picked up the ones she'd just finished frying. 'These are still nice and hot,' she said, carrying them over to the table.

'But . . .' I began.

'What?'

'Nothing,' I said.

Geena and Jazz sat down at the table, while Auntie chopped salad. I sat down too, although I wasn't planning to eat anything.

'Don't eat the samosas,' I said under my breath.

'What did you say?' asked Geena.

'Don't mutter, Amber.' Auntie brought a bowl of salad over to the table. 'It's rude.'

There was nothing I could do, honest. Geena and Jazz helped themselves to samosas. I ate a tomato and waited.

'Be careful,' Auntie warned, 'They're still quite hot.'

You don't know how hot, I thought.

Jazz and Geena took a big bite at the same moment. Jazz screamed and spat hers out across the table, just missing my eye. Geena spluttered, and spat hers onto her plate. They both grabbed the water jug and started fighting over it.

'Oh dear.' Auntie sat down at the table. 'I did warn you that they were hot.'

'*Hot!*' Geena roared, between gulps of water. 'They're scorching!'

'Too – *gulp* – much – *gulp* – pepper,' Jazz mumbled, fixing Auntie with a glare.

'Oh dear.' Auntie turned to look at me. She smiled widely, and I knew she knew. 'Aren't they the ones *you* made, Amber?'

'Oh, I don't think so,' I said airily, trying to bluff it out. 'All samosas look the same to me.'

Auntie bent over and picked a nail transfer out of the remains of Geena's samosa. 'Oh, really,' she said.

I looked down at my nails. I hadn't had time to varnish the transfers on properly. One was missing from my little finger.

Geena and Jazz stared at me. I could almost see their minds ticking over as they put two and two together. And I knew I was going to have to pay for it sometime. Probably quite soon.

'Sorry,' I muttered, as Auntie went to fetch more samosas.

Two shoes connected with my shins under the table.

'*Ow!*' I suppose I couldn't blame them, though.

'Here, try these.' Auntie handed round another plate of samosas. She smiled at me, and I could see the challenge in that smile. She thought she'd got the better of us, and so she had. This time. But although she'd won this particular battle, the war wasn't over yet. Not by a long way.

She made us go to bed at 10 p.m. that evening. Would you believe it? *And* she took the fuse out of the plug on Jazz's telly. Geena's, too. We were seething with rage. Dad hadn't come back from work yet, so we couldn't moan to him. That was why I was reading under the bedclothes with my torch, even though it was after midnight. *She* wasn't going to boss *me* around.

Jazz had said the same thing. But she had only lasted about half an hour before she fell asleep with her head in a book. She was snoring ever so slightly now, sprawled out with her knee in my back. She looked younger when she was asleep, more like how I remembered her looking years ago. Sweet, too. I wouldn't have told her that under torture.

'Amber?' Dad had pushed the door open, and was standing in the doorway. 'Why aren't you asleep?'

'Sorry,' I said, quickly switching off my torch.

Dad came further into the room. 'Everything all right?' He said it in a pleading kind of voice.

For once, I wanted to say no. Here, in the middle of the night, in the dark, with just the faintest glow from the landing light, maybe it was easier to be honest. I was desperate to ask him if he really wanted Auntie here at all. Or maybe *talking* would just start something I should keep away from at all costs.

'Everything's fine,' I said, and the moment passed.

'Good.' I could hear the relief in Dad's voice. He went out and closed the door.

It was a long time before I got to sleep.

CHAPTER 4

Everything continued to go spectacularly wrong. By Monday morning the three of us were ready to take our case to the European Court of Human Rights.

'She got me up at eight o'clock on Sunday morning to tidy my bedroom,' Geena exploded as we stalked out of the house. 'Eight o'clock on a Sunday morning. It's disgusting.'

'So's your bedroom,' Jazz sniggered, and got a clip round the ear for her trouble.

'You can wipe that grin off your face, Amber,' Jazz snorted, rubbing her ear. 'I heard Auntie telling Dad that no way are you getting new trainers when you've got six pairs already.'

'How does she know I've got six pairs?' I demanded. 'She must've been snooping around.'

'*And* she knows that you've got that Nike pair which cost eighty quid that you've never worn,' Jazz finished off triumphantly.

'They make my feet look big,' I retorted. 'And what's with the bedtimes? Bedtimes are for wimps. I can never get to sleep before midnight.'

'She came in last night at eleven to check that we were asleep,' said Jazz.

'Did she?' I frowned. 'I didn't notice.'

'You were asleep,' Jazz said with a smirk. 'I was only awake because you were snoring.'

'She's never going to leave us alone,' Geena said in dismay. 'She's going to be watching us every minute. It'll be like being stalked by the sari division of the SAS.'

We all glanced nervously over our shoulders. Auntie wasn't there, but Kim was, lumbering determinedly down the road towards us with her heavy bag.

'Hi,' she panted. 'Did you have a good weekend?'

'Well, our aunt arrived unexpectedly, and proceeded to make our lives a misery,' I said. 'What do you think?'

'Oh.' Kim looked puzzled. 'I thought she wasn't coming for a while.'

'So did we,' Geena said.

'What have you done to your head, Kim?' Jazz asked.

Kim put her hand up to the bruise on her temple. It was half-hidden by her floppy blonde hair. 'Oh, nothing.' She shrugged. 'I walked into a door.'

'Kim, you're so clumsy,' I said, amused. 'Did it hurt?'

'A bit,' she muttered sheepishly.

'Well, your weekend still couldn't have been as bad

as ours,' I went on. 'Auntie stuck her big fat nose into *everything.*'

'So what are we going to do about it?' demanded Geena.

'I don't know yet,' I said. 'But she's not getting away with it.'

School was a chance to forget about Auntie for a while, but you couldn't call it relaxing. All the teachers were infected with inspector fever. The symptoms were a worried look, a frantic manner and a tendency to freak out at regular intervals. We'd only been in our form room for ten minutes, and by the time the assembly bell rang, Mr Arora had already handed out four detentions. George Botley got three of them.

Assembly was Mr Grimwade reading out the booklet of school rules in a deadly, monotonous voice. This was accompanied by many, varied threats about what would happen to us if we didn't behave while the inspectors were here. Then it was off to classes, where all the teachers immediately set us work to do, while they sat and wrote notes all through the lesson. Geena said it was because they had to have files of lesson plans to show the inspectors, and a lot of them had fallen behind. There was a rumour going round that Mr Lucas, who taught history, hadn't written down any lesson plans for the last six months, and was having to make them all up. Chelsea said someone had told her that Miss Patel

59

was going to pretend hers had been stolen.

There was a meeting at lunch time about the over-the-top assembly, which was to impress the inspectors. Jazz, Geena and I went across the road to the new school hall, which was an amazing construction of glass, steel and concrete with a huge stage at one end of it.

Ms Woods, the drama teacher who was organizing the assembly, was rushing round the hall with a tragic face. She fell on us as if we were her long-lost daughters.

'At last,' she declared, sweeping her big, black hair off her face. 'Someone I can actually rely on.'

We smiled calm and trustworthy smiles.

'What would you like us to do, Ms Woods?' Geena asked in a business-like manner.

'Anything and everything,' Ms Woods replied. 'There's plenty of scenery to be painted, and I need someone to operate the CD player and the overhead projector, as well as change the scenery. And, of course, you'll be taking part in the assembly itself.'

Of course.

'The trouble is, the feng shui in here is all wrong.' Ms Woods looked round the hall in a demented way. 'It ought to be *completely* rebuilt from scratch.'

We stood there in polite silence. Ms Woods would just have to accept that it was unlikely that the brand-new school hall could be knocked down and rebuilt before the inspectors arrived.

'Right, this is the plan.' Ms Woods fought her way through mounds of paper in her bag and pulled out a list. 'The six major religions of the world will each be represented by words, music and a specially painted backdrop. So the Buddhist section will have a large golden Buddha, the Christian section will have a church and so on. And,' she went on, dropping the list on the floor and scrambling to retrieve it, 'I thought it would be fantastic if each religion were represented by pupils who actually practise it at home.'

'Where's she going to find a Buddhist at Coppergate?' Geena whispered in my ear.

'Now, as you three girls are . . .' Ms Woods squinted at us as if our religion were branded on our foreheads.

'Sikhs,' I said helpfully.

'Yes. Exactly.' Ms Woods looked relieved. 'I thought we'd have a large scenic backdrop of the Golden Temple. The three of you will stand in front of it, and read out some information about Sikhism.'

'Fine,' Geena agreed. 'And we can look after the tape recorder and the overhead projector too, if you want.'

'Oh, would you?' Ms Woods looked pathetically relieved. 'I know I can trust *you*.'

'No problem,' the three of us said together.

'By the way,' Ms Woods went on with manic desperation, 'you don't happen to know any Buddhists, do you?'

*

Ever since I could remember, we'd visited relatives on a Sunday, or they'd come to visit us. Last week Auntie had only just arrived so we'd stayed at home, but today we had a lot of calls to make because everyone wanted to see her.

'Although God knows why,' Geena said. She eyed herself critically in Jazz's mirror. We were all wearing the latest suits from the sari shop, which were long, swirly skirts with a tight, short top and a floaty scarf. Mine was silver, Jazz's was pink and Geena's was lilac. Visiting the family was definitely an Indian clothes day. We could have given some of our elderly relatives a heart attack if we'd turned up in miniskirts.

'This is our chance,' I said, sticking a silver bindi on my forehead. 'We can get our own back.'

'Ooh, how?' Jazz demanded, looking excited.

'I don't know,' I said. 'But we'll think of something.'

Auntie and Dad were waiting for us in the car. Auntie looked all right, I suppose. She was wearing a purple sari with silver embroidery, and she had her hair up. I don't know why it annoyed me that she looked pretty, but it did.

'Where are we going first, Dad?' Jazz asked, as he whizzed us onto the dual carriageway.

'Uncle Davinder's,' Dad replied.

We groaned. Uncle Davinder, or Uncle Dave as he liked us to call him, was Dad's cousin or something.

No one had ever explained to us exactly who all our relations were because it was far too complicated. It was just possible that we weren't actually related at all. Anyway, Uncle Dave, who was a laugh, was married to Auntie Rita, who was a pain. They had four children – three boys, who were all right, and a girl called Poonam, who was known as Baby. That also annoyed me, because she was fifteen years old. She was a pain, too.

'Is Rita the same as ever?' Auntie asked. We were pulling up outside their six-bedroom, detached house with landscaped gardens.

Dad sighed. 'Oh, yes.'

'Oh dear.' Auntie's face fell as she got out of the car.

'Rita, *darling*, how are you?' she gushed, as the front door opened. 'My God, it's been *years*.'

Uncle Dave and Auntie Rita rushed out and there was a lot of hugging. Uncle Dave's tall and thin and likes slobbing around in kurta pyjamas, but today Auntie Rita had forced him into a smart suit. He pinched my cheek hard, as usual, even though I tried to hide behind Geena.

'Hello, Amber, how are you?' he beamed.

'All right, but I might need a doctor,' I said, massaging my throbbing cheek.

Uncle Dave roared with laughter, and attacked Jazz from the side, when she was least expecting it.

'It's wonderful to see you.' Auntie Rita was over-dressed, as usual. She wore a pink and purple sari, and gold everywhere, and her hair was hoisted into position and armoured with about three cans of hairspray. 'Before we go inside, you must have a look at our new Mercedes.' She tucked her arm into Auntie's, and waved at the gleaming silver car sitting in the driveway. 'It's got everything. Air-conditioning, a computer, a fridge. Even a mini TV.'

We all admired the car. Then we trooped into the house, where Auntie Rita pointed out the new curtains from Harrods and all the furniture they'd bought over the last six months.

Baby was sitting with Biji, her gran, in the enormous living room. I forgot to say that Biji lives with Uncle Dave and Auntie Rita. I don't need to tell you anything about Biji. You'll see what she's like in about two seconds.

'You've put on weight,' Biji remarked, giving Auntie a hug.

'Thank you,' Auntie said dryly.

'The boys have gone out, but you remember Baby.' Auntie Rita pointed at Poonam proudly. 'She's so grown up now, but still such a good girl.'

'Hello, Auntie,' Baby said sweetly. She looked as if butter wouldn't melt in her mouth, with her long plaits and her red suit. She didn't know that Geena and I had seen her in the High Street last week, flirting with some boy outside Woolworths, wearing a skirt up to her bottom. I bet Auntie Rita didn't know about *that*.

'You look tired.' Biji stared accusingly at Dad. 'Haggard. Baggy-eyed. Not surprising really, considering.'

'I'm fine,' Dad said defensively.

Everyone looked embarrassed, except Biji, of course.

Uncle Dave cleared his throat, and clapped Dad on the shoulder. 'Let's go next door, and leave the women to it,' he suggested. He did this every time we visited. He and Dad would go into the study and drink whisky, and then they'd have a chilli-eating contest. Dad always lost, and had to spend the next three hours drinking loads of water.

'Now who's for tea?' Auntie Rita said brightly, bustling off to the kitchen.

Jazz groaned. 'Oh no, do we *have* to?' she said under her breath.

Auntie Rita makes the most revolting tea. She does it the Indian way, which means boiling up the tea leaves with cardamom seeds and adding loads of sugar. It tastes disgusting.

Auntie glared at us. 'You'll drink what you're given,' she snapped in a low voice.

I stared thoughtfully at Auntie. She was definitely uptight and nervous. Auntie Rita has that effect on people. It was something that could be used to our advantage.

'Is that the same suit you wore to Lalita's wedding, Amber?' Baby asked me sweetly, looking me over as if I was something the cat had brought up. 'It still looks nice, even though it's so *old*.'

I smiled. 'Didn't Geena and I see you outside Woolworths last week?'

Baby turned as red as her shalwar kameez and shut up.

'Here we are.' Auntie Rita staggered in, carrying an enormous silver teapot and posh china cups and saucers on a tray.

The tea was as horrible as it always was. It was so strong, it looked as if it had solidified.

'This tea isn't strong enough,' Biji moaned. She pulled her white sari over her head grumpily. 'I'm an old woman. Can't I have my tea the way I like it?'

Auntie Rita gritted her teeth and handed me my cup. I stared down at the treacle-brown liquid, wondering which technique I should go for this time. There were two. I could either take really small sips, and hope the taste didn't come through too much, or I could really go for it, and take big gulps. From the disgusted look on Jazz's face, she was going for the quick-gulps-and-get-it-over-with technique. Geena was sipping steadily, and shuddering every so often.

'You'll have to give us all the news from India, Susie,' Auntie Rita said. 'How are Mohan, Palvinder and the kids?' But she didn't wait for an answer. 'Did I tell you Jaggi's got into Cambridge University? We're so proud of him. He's going to study law. And Sukhvinder's doing really well at medical school.

Bobby's just been promoted at the engineering company, too.'

'Lovely,' Auntie said.

Doctor. Lawyer. Accountant. Teacher. Engineer. Pharmacist. They were all good careers for good Indian boys and girls. Careers their parents could boast about.

'And Baby's doing really well at school,' Auntie Rita went on. 'She wants to be a lawyer like her brother, don't you, *beti*?'

'Until she gets married and has children, of course,' Biji interjected grumpily. She fixed me, Geena and Jazz with a piercing stare. 'How are you getting on at school? I hope you're not wasting your time running around with *boys*.' She made them sound like a fatal disease.

'We're doing all right, Biji,' Geena replied politely.

'Oh, don't be so modest, Geena,' Auntie cut in. I could tell she wanted to show off about us too. 'Your father tells me you're all doing really well. Your reports were excellent.'

I saw my chance. I shrugged. 'They were all right,' I said. 'But it doesn't really matter anyway.'

Biji sat up ramrod straight. 'What do you mean, "It doesn't matter," child?' she snapped. 'How will you find a good husband if you don't get yourself a decent education?'

'I don't want to get married,' I said.

You'd have thought I'd said I'd murdered someone.

57

Auntie Rita gasped and nearly dropped the teapot. Biji goggled at me from behind her five-centimetre-thick glasses. Even Auntie looked shocked. I went for the killer touch.

'I want to be a pop star,' I added.

Biji almost fell off the sofa. 'A *pop star*?' she screeched. 'What kind of a job is *that* for a respectable Indian girl?'

Auntie glared at me. She looked seriously embar-rassed, and I was glad. 'Be quiet, Amber,' she hissed.

'But I *do* want to be a pop star,' I insisted. I was enjoying myself. 'Why not?'

'What do you mean, "Why not"?' Biji was clutching her heart dramatically. 'Dancing around in skimpy clothes, singing suggestive songs? Your father wouldn't allow it.'

'He can't stop me,' I said coolly.

Auntie looked as if she wanted to throttle me. I didn't really want to be a pop star. Well, I wouldn't have minded, but I can't sing. I mean, I *really* can't sing. I sound like a bunch of cats having their tails pulled.

'I've never heard anything so ridiculous in my life,' Auntie Rita declared, patting her rock-hard hairdo. 'You'll have to knock these silly ideas out of her head, Susie.'

I glanced at Geena and Jazz. They were smiling. They were enjoying seeing Auntie squirm as much as I was.

Auntie was watching me closely, and I tried to meet her gaze without looking too triumphant. Then, after a moment, she shrugged. 'Well, if that's what Amber really wants . . .'

What? I blinked. She wasn't supposed to say that.

'What do you mean?' Biji howled, slowly turning purple. 'No relative of mine is going to be a pop star!'

'But if Amber's got a good voice, and that's what she wants to do, well, maybe there's no harm in it,' Auntie said thoughtfully. To my utter horror, I was beginning to get an idea of where she was going with this. 'Perhaps she *has* got a good voice.' She stared coolly at me. 'I wouldn't know. I've never heard her sing.'

'Oh, my voice isn't that great,' I said quickly.

'Why don't you let us be the judge of that?' Auntie folded her arms. 'Go on. Sing something for us now.'

'S-s-s-s-sing?' I stuttered.

'Yes.' Auntie fixed me with a steely stare. 'Now.'

'That's a good idea,' Baby chimed in. I could almost see a big, flashing sign saying REVENGE! above her head. 'Shall I go and get Dad and Uncle Johnny?'

'No, don't do that,' I said. But Baby had already whisked out of the room.

'Ah, here come the boys.' Auntie Rita beamed, as the front door opened. 'I'm sure they'd like to hear Amber sing too.'

Geena and Jazz were looking at me sympathetically. I swallowed hard. I glared at Auntie, who stared serenely back at me. She needn't think she'd got the better of me. I'd show her. Oh, yes.

'That,' I said heavily, flinging myself onto Jazz's bed, 'was just about the most embarrassing thing I've ever had to live through.'

'I thought that was the day you started school,' Geena remarked, following me into the room. 'You know, when you wet yourself and it went all over the teacher's shoes.'

'Forget that,' I groaned, burying my face in a pillow. 'Today overtook it by miles.' I cringed as I remembered my terrible rendition of Kylie's latest single. Even Biji had been laughing by the end of it.

'It was all Auntie's fault,' I went on bitterly. 'She set me up.'

'And you fell into it,' Jazz pointed out helpfully. '*Right* into it.'

'Thank you.' I hurled a pillow at her, and felt better when it smacked her in the face. 'Now I've got to get my own back.'

'How?' Geena asked.

I didn't know. I'd spent the rest of the day keeping my mouth firmly shut, while we went on visiting people, and I hadn't come up with anything. But suddenly an idea swam right into my head from nowhere. It was *beautiful*.

'I've got it,' I said. 'We'll pierce Jazz's ears.'

'I beg your pardon?' Jazz spluttered.

'We'll pierce your ears,' I repeated. 'We'll do it our-selves. Right now. That'll show her.'

Geena grinned. 'Great idea, Amber.'

'Hold on a minute.' Jazz wasn't looking very enthusiastic. 'Exactly *how* are you going to do that?'

'With a pin,' I said. 'We'll sterilize it in disinfectant first, so you don't catch anything nasty.'

Jazz frowned. 'But it'll *hurt*.'

'No, it won't,' I said. 'We'll numb your ears first with some ice from the freezer. It won't hurt a bit.'

'Can't I just go into town after school tomorrow, and get my ears pierced in Claire's Accessories?' Jazz pleaded.

I shook my head. 'Come on, Jazz,' I said. 'Don't be a baby. It's a perfect way to show Auntie that she can't boss us around.'

'Yes, except that it involves pain,' Jazz grumbled. '*My* pain. And what about Dad?'

'I didn't think of that.' Geena glanced at me. 'Dad will kill us, Amber.'

I shrugged. 'He'll get over it.' I wasn't about to give up my brilliant idea. Auntie had defeated us on all fronts so far, and anyway, Dad had one foot in the enemy camp now. 'Come on, Jazz,' I coaxed her. 'You really want those second holes, don't you?'

Jazz was wavering. 'Well, yes . . .'

'And I promise you it won't hurt,' I went on, crossing my fingers behind my back.

'All right then.'

'Yes!' I slapped Jazz's shoulder. 'You go and get the ice, and Geena and I will organize everything else.'

'Make sure it's a really small pin,' Jazz ordered us, going over to the door.

'Sure,' I agreed. 'Get the biggest needle you can find,' I said under my breath to Geena. 'It won't work otherwise.'

By the time Jazz came back, we had everything sorted. Geena had found a gigantic needle, which we'd put in a tooth mug of Dettol and hidden behind a pile of books. We didn't want Jazz to freak out.

'Where's the ice?' I asked. Jazz had a family pack of frozen peas in her hand.

'There wasn't any,' she said. 'I thought this would do instead.'

'All right, sit on the bed and stick it on your ear,' I instructed her.

'Ow, it's cold,' Jazz complained, clapping the frozen peas to the side of her head. 'Where's the pin?'

'Don't worry about that,' I said, advancing towards her. I touched her ear. 'Now, relax. I'm just going to—'

'*Aargh!*' Jazz screeched, pulling away from me.

'I'm just marking some dots on your ear with a biro, you idiot. Look.' I dangled the pen under her nose. 'I haven't even started yet.'

'I'll put a CD on,' Geena said. 'That'll help you to relax, Jazz.' She raised her eyebrows at me. 'And it'll muffle the screams,' she whispered.

Geena put a Coldplay CD on, and I marked two

dots on Jazz's ears, using the first holes as a guide. It was difficult to get the dots in the right place, but it wouldn't be too noticeable if the holes weren't quite level. I hoped. Then I took the giant needle out of the disinfectant.

'Close your eyes, Jazz,' I said, keeping it behind my back.

Jazz did as she was told. I squinted down at her left ear. I was aiming the needle at the biro mark, when the bedroom door opened.

'I've made some tea—' Auntie began.

Several things happened. Jazz opened her eyes, saw the size of the needle and let out a hysterical scream. I almost jumped out of my skin. The needle flew out of my hand and across the room, straight towards Geena like an arrow. She leaped backwards, and knocked the tooth mug of disinfectant over the CD player. Coldplay ground to a watery, shuddering halt.

'What are you doing?' Auntie asked in quite a reasonable tone of voice, considering.

'We're piercing Jazz's ears, Auntie,' Geena replied politely.

'Oh.' Auntie advanced into the room, and folded her arms. I waited for her to go mental. 'Better get on with it, then.'

'I'm sorry?' I said, hardly believing my ears.

Auntie shrugged. 'I said, you'd better get on with it. Tea's ready.'

Oh, it was perfectly obvious what she was up to. She was trying to call our bluff. Like it was *really* going to work.

'All right,' I said. 'Get ready, Jazz.'

'But—' Jazz began, eyeing the needle.

'*Now*,' I said sternly.

Reluctantly Jazz stuck the frozen peas on her left ear again, and Geena handed me the needle. We all ignored Auntie. She was still standing there, trying to put us off.

'That's a big needle,' she said, as I held it over Jazz's left ear.

Jazz squinted sideways at the needle. I glared at her.

'It's going to hurt,' Auntie went on, standing there like some prophet of doom in a sari. 'I mean, *really* hurt.'

'She's just trying it on,' I whispered to Jazz. 'Take no notice.'

'I had my ears pierced with a needle when I was a kid,' Auntie went on. 'That's the way they do it in India, back home in the village, you know. That's why I can tell you for sure that it hurts like mad.'

'OK, Jazz,' I said brightly. 'Here we go.'

'One of my friends, Sarbjit, had hers done at the same time as me.' Auntie examined her fingernails. 'She must have caught an infection because her ears swelled right up. The other kids called her Dumbo for weeks.'

'Forget it!' Jazz howled. She jumped to her feet and knocked my arm away. 'I'm not having it done. No way.'

Auntie went over to the door. 'Tea's ready, don't forget.' She waltzed out, humming a song from *Reena aur Meena*.

'Jazz, you complete prat,' I hissed. 'That was exactly what she *wanted* you to do.'

'I don't care,' Jazz said sulkily, clapping her hands over her ears. 'I'm not going around looking like Dumbo the elephant.'

'Look, maybe it wasn't such a good idea, anyway,' Geena said, jumping in between us before we started thumping each other. 'It would've got us into big trouble with Dad.'

'So Auntie's won again,' I said bitterly. Whatever we did, she got the better of us every time. I couldn't see any way out of it.

'There's nothing else for it,' Geena said. 'She's got to go. Any ideas?'

We all flopped onto the bed. We lay there in a row, kicking our legs against the headboard, thinking. It seemed an impossible situation. Auntie was here to stay. There was no reason why she would go back to India. Her parents, our grandparents, were dead, so she didn't have any close family there. Most of her relatives were in England, unluckily. I supposed she might get married one day and leave. Or at her age she might not get married at all, and we'd be stuck

75

with her until *we* left home. It was a totally depressing thought.

Then I smiled. Call me a genius.

'I've got it,' I said.

CHAPTER 5

'An *arranged* marriage?' Geena stared at me.

I nodded.

'Arranged by *us*?' Jazz's eyes were round as dinner plates.

I nodded again. 'We find a husband for Auntie, get her married off and get rid of her. It's perfect.'

Geena and Jazz didn't seem to think so. They were looking distinctly doubtful.

'We've got to find someone who'll have her, first,' Jazz pointed out.

'*That* won't be easy,' Geena remarked.

'If anyone's got a better idea,' I snapped, 'just say so.'

There was silence.

'So it's agreed then,' I went on. 'We look for someone daft enough to marry Auntie.'

'Exactly *how* are we going to do that?' Geena asked. 'Stop suitable husbands in the street, and beg them to propose?'

'We could put an ad in the newspaper,' Jazz suggested. '*Wanted: one man daft enough to marry a bossy, interfering aunt.*'

'We could hold a raffle,' Geena added. 'The winner gets Auntie.'

'Or the loser,' Jazz said, and they both giggled.

'Oh, behave,' I said. 'I thought we'd try Mrs Dhaliwal.'

Mrs Dhaliwal lived a few streets away, and her mission in life was to get people married off. She always carried a huge file, which was full of the photos and personal details of people who were looking for husbands and wives, and she'd show it around at every possible opportunity. Mrs D could smell an unmarried person a mile off. In fact, I was surprised she hadn't homed in on Auntie already.

'And what do we say to her?' Jazz asked.

'Nothing much,' I replied. 'We just get her to come round for tea: she'll bring her file because she always does, and then we're away.'

'It can't possibly be that simple,' Jazz said doubtfully.

And, of course, it wasn't.

The first thing we had to do was get our hands on Mrs Dhaliwal. Even though she only lived a couple of streets away, she was really hard to pin down because she was second only to Auntie in the interfering stakes. If she wasn't in the minimarket telling Mr Attwal how to arrange his shelves, then she was visiting all the Indian families in the area, trying to arrange marriages. We didn't want to knock on her door and just invite her over, because that would have looked too suspicious. And anyway, she was never in.

It took us four days of hanging around and stalking Mrs Dhaliwal's family to find out her movements, and by the end of it we were three nervous wrecks. It was another bad week, too. At school, a stressed-out Ms Woods threw a fit and announced that the assembly would not be taking place. Rumour had it that Mr Grimwade had to get down on his bended knees to get her to change her mind. At home, Auntie was sweeping through the place like a tornado, destroying everything in her path. She was really going for the unpopularity vote.

One night Geena had had a stand-up row with Auntie over the time she'd got back from a mate's house and had then got into trouble with Dad too when Auntie snitched on her. Geena was prepared to murder her, and Jazz and I were quite ready to help with the disposal of the body. These were desperate times.

'Here comes Mrs D,' Geena whispered.

We popped out from behind our hedge. We were on our way to school, but we'd been hiding there for the last ten minutes, waiting for Mrs Dhaliwal to come along. We'd discovered that she'd just started a part-time job in the local library. It hadn't been easy finding out which shifts she worked, but we'd managed it, thanks to Geena chatting up Mrs D's son.

Mrs Dhaliwal was walking briskly along the road,

her green sari swishing around her ankles. She was tall and square, and she wore her hair up in a fat bun, like a cottage loaf. Jazz said she had antennae hidden under there which beamed in on people who weren't married.

'Hello, girls,' Mrs Dhaliwal beamed. 'On your way to school?'

We smiled and nodded.

'I hear your aunt's staying with you,' she went on eagerly.

I swear I saw that huge bun of hair twitch.

'Yes, she is,' Jazz agreed.

'And your father tells me she's not married yet,' Mrs Dhaliwal went on. She smiled widely, a cat preparing to pounce on a mouse.

'No, she isn't,' I said. 'And she'd *love* to meet you.'

'Why don't you pop round and say hello to Auntie?' Geena suggested.

'I'll do that,' Mrs Dhaliwal said. There was a faraway look in her eyes, and I guessed that she was running through her file of possible candidates. With any luck, she'd find the perfect match. Then our troubles would be over.

'Yes!' Jazz said with satisfaction, as Mrs Dhaliwal went on her way. 'Auntie won't know what's hit her.'

'Amber, wait for me!' Kim was rushing down the street towards us.

'How's things?' she asked. 'Is your Auntie still getting on your nerves?'

'Is the grass green?' replied Geena.

'But we've got a plan to get rid of her,' Jazz added. 'We're going to find her a husband.'

Kim looked confused as she took that in. 'But what if she doesn't want to get married?'

'Of course she does,' I said with more confidence than I felt. 'She probably just hasn't found anyone dumb enough to marry her yet.'

'But you can't *make* her get married if she doesn't want to—' Kim began.

'Indian girls get married, Kim,' I said impatiently. 'It's what they *do*. Everyone expects it.'

'Sarika Sharma didn't,' Geena remarked. 'You know, my friend Kamini's sister? She's got that amazing job with Microsoft, and a posh penthouse in Canary Wharf.'

'And what about Razia Khan?' Jazz said. 'She's a lawyer, and *she's* not married.'

'All right,' I retorted. 'So they haven't got married *yet*. But they probably will. We're just hurrying Auntie up a bit, that's all.' I played my ace card. 'And if no one's got a better idea . . .'

Nobody had.

As the inspectors' visit drew nearer, panicking had become a daily activity at school. I honestly don't know how the teachers would have managed without us three. We spent every lunch time helping Ms Woods design and paint the backdrops for the assembly. And calming her down each time she got upset, which was often. I didn't do PE that afternoon. Instead I spent the lesson helping Mr Arora to tidy up the lower school maths cupboard, just in case the inspectors inspected it. Geena was outside the school office, painting a mural on the wall which said WELCOME in about forty different languages. It covered up the cracks really well. Meanwhile, Mr Grimwade had Jazz going round the lower school for most of the afternoon, delivering messages and threats about the coming visit.

'They should let the three of *us* run the school,' I said, as we walked home that afternoon. 'Then there'd be no problems.'

'True,' Geena agreed.

Jazz was staring down the street at the minimarket, which was just ahead of us. 'I think I'm seeing things,' she said in a dazed voice. 'What's Mr Attwal doing?'

It was all very strange. Mr Attwal was sitting outside the shop on a chair. He did that sometimes if the weather was fine and sunny, as it was today. He could pounce on passers-by and lure them into conversation more easily then. But today Mr Attwal was reading some kind of leaflet or pamphlet. What it was, we couldn't see from here. But it was so interesting, he never once raised his head. Not even when a load of schoolboys went into the shop, one after the other.

'What's going on?' Jazz wanted to know.

We were all quite curious. We went up to Mr Attwal and stood in front of him. Eventually he looked up, but only because we were casting a shadow across him.

He blinked. 'Hello, girls.'

'What are you reading?' Geena asked. But we could see what the leaflet was. *Want to learn about computers? Want to learn a language? Fulfil your potential with our CORRESPONDENCE COURSES!* There was a large pile of similar leaflets beside him.

Mr Attwal's round face lit up. 'I'm going back to school,' he said triumphantly. 'Well, not really. I still have to look after the shop. But that's why a correspondence course is perfect for me.'

'What are you going to learn?' Geena asked.

He shrugged. 'There are so many things. Book-keeping, computers, engineering, languages. I haven't made my mind up yet.'

'That's great,' I said, meaning it. It certainly solved the problem of him boring all his customers to death. But I couldn't help wondering why he hadn't thought of it years ago.

'Actually, it was your auntie who gave me the idea,' Mr Attwal said happily.

'*Auntie?*' I repeated.

'Yes, she came into the shop and we got talking, and she said what about a correspondence course?' Mr Attwal went on. 'So I left my wife looking after the shop, went to the library and got these leaflets. Your auntie's a very clever lady.'

Clever wasn't the word I was thinking of.

'Now I can be whatever I want to be,' Mr Attwal said. His eyes were dreamy.

We walked on. We were stunned.

'I don't believe it,' I muttered. 'Now she's interfering in the neighbours' lives as well as ours.'

'She's so *nosy*,' Jazz said. 'Why can't she mind her own business?'

'Because she just has to interfere, wherever she goes,' Geena snapped. 'She's a professional nosy parker.'

We were furious. None of us wanted to point out that maybe it was a good thing for Mr Attwal and his customers that Auntie had interfered. She shouldn't have interfered *at all*.

'She's obviously not satisfied with running *our* lives,' I said moodily. I walked along the gutter, kicking an empty Coke can. 'She's branching out into the whole community.'

'Amber, look out!' Geena grabbed my arm and hauled me onto the pavement. A millisecond later the paperboy cycled past like a demon. He was grinning all over his face.

'I'm going to *kill* him,' I said through my teeth. I was totally fed up, and someone was going to suffer. The paperboy seemed like the perfect victim.

I threw my bag at Geena and raced after him. He

hurled the evening newspaper first into our porch, and then into Mrs Macey's. But before I could even get near him, he stood up on the pedals and cycled off.

Suddenly Mrs Macey's front door flew open. She stood there, red in the face, and she shook her fist at the paperboy's back. I've never actually *seen* anyone do that before.

Then she noticed me panting at our gate. She glared at me, muttered something about us 'all being the same', went back in and slammed the door.

'Miserable old bag,' I muttered. It was obvious what she meant, about us 'all being the same'. Obvious, because the paperboy was black.

Geena and Jazz joined me.

'What is her problem?' Jazz asked.

I shrugged. It wasn't worth worrying about. We'd always suspected Mrs Macey didn't like us because we were Indian. Now we knew for certain.

When we let ourselves into the house, we could hear voices from the living room. Auntie and Mrs Dhaliwal. Already. We hadn't expected things to move quite so fast.

Mrs Dhaliwal was sitting comfortably on the sofa. She had a cup of tea in one hand, and a biscuit in the other. Her file of marriage partners lay on her knees.

'We've been waiting for you, girls,' Auntie declared easily. She didn't look cross or upset. If anything, she looked pink-cheeked and pleased. My heart lifted.

Maybe she really did want to get married after all. Oh, this was going to be so easy.

We each got a cup of tea and sat down. I wasn't quite sure how to bring up the subject of husbands. But as it turned out, I didn't need to.

'Right, shall we get started then?' Mrs Dhaliwal asked eagerly.

'Yes, let's,' Auntie agreed, looking just as enthusiastic.

I grinned at Geena and Jazz. None of us could believe it was going so well.

'What about your brother, though?' Mrs Dhaliwal frowned at Auntie. 'Shouldn't we wait until he comes home?'

I pulled a face at Geena and Jazz.

'Oh, I don't think so.' Auntie glanced at us, as if she was looking for our support. 'We're all modern, liberated women here. I'm sure my brother will back any decision we make.'

'Absolutely, Auntie,' Geena said firmly. Jazz and I nodded.

Mrs Dhaliwal beamed. 'Well, here we go.' She opened up the file, and pulled out a photo. 'What kind of age range are we looking at? I suppose you don't want anyone too old?'

'I'm not sure.' Auntie stroked her chin. 'What do you think, Geena?'

'Well, up to fifty would be all right,' Geena replied. She winked at us. I knew what she was thinking. We needed the widest possible range of husbands to choose from to make sure we found someone.

Auntie raised her eyebrows. She looked a bit shocked, but all she said was, 'Well, if you're sure . . .'

'Here's one.' Mrs Dhaliwal passed the photo to Auntie. 'Jagdev Singh. What do you think?'

Auntie looked at the photo without comment, then passed it to Geena.

'What's that big lump on the end of his nose?' Geena asked.

I took a look.

'That *is* his nose,' I said. The poor man was hideous.

Jazz looked at the photo and shrieked with laughter, then had to turn it into a cough.

'He's got a very good job,' Mrs Dhaliwal said huffily. 'He's an accountant.'

'Yes, I'm sure he's very good at sniffing out tax scams,' Geena said solemnly. I don't know how she managed to keep a straight face.

Mrs Dhaliwal took out another photo, and handed it to Auntie. 'What about this one?'

'Yes, well . . .' Auntie didn't look impressed. 'He's rather *large*, isn't he?'

That was an understatement. This guy was huge.

'Who ate all the samosas?' Jazz whispered in my ear. We both nearly burst, trying not to laugh.

'What do you think, Geena?' Auntie asked.

'Well, if you want my honest opinion, Auntie –' I

could tell that Geena was starting to enjoy herself – 'I really think that personality is *much* more important than looks.'

'Very true.' Auntie nodded. 'So he's a possibility then?'

Geena smiled. 'Oh, definitely.'

'Now here's a good one,' Mrs Dhaliwal said proudly. 'He works at the BBC.'

She forgot to mention that he also had no hair on his head, but a lot growing out of his nose. By this time Jazz was in such hysterics, she had to dash to the loo. I was only just managing to hold myself together by biting the inside of my mouth really hard. But Geena was going great guns.

'He's got a kind face,' she remarked.

'Oh, do you think so?' Auntie said doubtfully.

'Personality, not looks, remember, Auntie,' Geena reminded her briskly.

Over the next hour, we saw it all. Acne, warts, jug-ears, strange shapes and sizes. I was beginning to wonder if Mrs Dhaliwal had any normal-looking people in her file.

'Well, we have a few possibilities here,' Auntie announced, sifting through the photographs again.

'If you're desperate,' I whispered in Jazz's ear. That set the two of us off again.

'I'll have to speak to Geena's father first, before we can go any further,' Auntie went on. 'Then we can meet the young man's family and discuss arrangements for the wedding. Of course, we'll have to wait until Geena's sixteen.'

Jazz and I stopped laughing.

'Excuse me?' Geena said faintly.

Auntie looked surprised. 'Well, you can't get married before you're sixteen, dear. That's the law here.'

'Who said anything about me getting married?' Geena snarled.

Auntie raised her eyebrows. 'Well, isn't that what all this is about?'

'*No*,' Geena said through her teeth. '*I'm* not getting married.'

'Oh.' Auntie looked puzzled. I couldn't tell if it was genuine, or if she was faking it. 'I thought that was why we were doing all this.'

'No, of *course* it isn't—' Geena began furiously. I shot her a warning look, and she shut up. I wasn't sure if Auntie was onto us, or if she'd made a genuine mistake. We didn't want to give the game away.

'Well, I'm glad we got that sorted out.' Auntie picked up our empty cups. 'More tea, anyone?'

And she went out.

Mrs Dhaliwal started packing the photos away, looking faintly disgruntled. I had to do something, and fast.

'Did Auntie say anything about looking for a husband herself?' I asked hopefully.

'Don't be silly, Amber.' Mrs Dhaliwal wagged her finger at me. 'How can your Auntie get married? She has to look after the three of you. She hasn't got time for a husband at the moment.'

So Auntie had even got Mrs Dhaliwal on her side. But I wasn't going to give up. One way or another, we'd just have to find her a husband ourselves. And soon.

CHAPTER 6

'Look, anyone will do,' Geena said. 'Come on, you must know *someone*.'

Chelsea looked doubtful. 'Well, there's our neighbour,' she said. 'He lives on his own. But he's got a wooden leg.'

'We're not fussy,' Jazz chimed in.

'How old is he?' I asked.

Chelsea screwed up her nose. 'About sixty?' she guessed.

'That's too old,' Geena grumbled, tapping her fingers impatiently on her clipboard. 'Don't you know anyone else?'

Chelsea shook her head and escaped across the playground, a look of relief on her face. I glanced round to see where Sharelle had got to. She was sidling off behind the bike sheds.

'What about your Uncle Mac, Sharelle?' I reminded her. 'You said he wasn't married.'

'Yeah, but he likes living on his own,' Sharelle said apologetically. 'And he's a bit strange. He collects bus tickets and files them. Anyway, he's not Indian.'

'At the moment we'd consider a little green man from Mars,' snapped Geena. 'Anyone else?'

Sharelle looked blank.

'Oh, this is hopeless,' I said. The campaign to find Auntie a husband had got off to a standing start.

'Hey, you.' Geena collared Ragbir Singh from Year 7. 'Do you know anyone who wants to get married?'

Ragbir backed away across the playground, giggling nervously.

'Not to me, you fool,' Geena snapped.

Ragbir giggled even harder. He took to his heels and vanished behind the canteen.

'Now it's going to be all round the school that Geena's looking for a husband,' Jazz remarked, trying not to sound gleeful but not trying very hard.

Geena gave us both a penetrating look. 'Well, I hope you'll put paid to *that* particular rumour if you hear it flying about.'

'Of course,' I said. 'After all, aren't you promised to Jagdev Singh the nosy accountant?'

Jazz and I collapsed in hysterics. Geena glared and waved the clipboard at us threateningly.

'Look, here's Kim,' Jazz gulped through her giggles.

'Oops,' I said. 'We forgot to wait for her this morning.'

'You forgot to wait for me this morning,' Kim complained, heaving her rucksack across the playground. She had a large plaster on her right hand which I deliberately didn't comment on. I didn't want to be bored to death for the next fifteen minutes.

'Sorry,' I said. 'We had something important to do.'

'We're trying to find a husband for Auntie,' Geena explained briskly. 'Do you know anyone?'

Kim looked glum. 'You could have Gary, if you like.'

'Gary?' I had to think for a minute to work out who she meant. 'Oh, your mum's boyfriend.'

Kim's eyes shadowed. 'I wouldn't mind getting rid of him,' she muttered.

I didn't ask what she meant because I didn't want to know. I had my own problems. And Kim was just so good at making a drama out of nothing.

'Make sure you ask everyone in your classes about husbands,' Geena ordered as the bell went.

'Yes, mein Führer.' Jazz goose-stepped into the Year 7 cloakroom.

'Geena,' Sarika Sharma called, 'someone says you're looking for a husband. Is that true?'

'Oh God,' Geena moaned.

An interested crowd began to gather, and some of the boys started making very rude jokes which I couldn't possibly repeat. They were funny, though.

'Of course she's not looking for a husband,' I said. 'She's already promised to Jagdev Singh.'

An enraged Geena made a run at me, and I disappeared, laughing, round the corner towards our classroom. Kim trailed along behind me, her eyes like saucers.

'Is Geena *really* getting married?' she asked.

'Kim, keep up for God's sake,' I snapped. 'Of course she isn't.'

'Oh.' Kim looked vaguely disappointed. Then she winced as something hit her on the back of the head. 'Help!'

I bent down and retrieved a woolly hat which had been balled up and used as a weapon. A few metres behind us George Botley was grinning like a maniac.

'Ignore him,' I said, dropping the hat into a nearby litter bin. It landed very satisfactorily on a half-eaten ice cream.

I sized up the rest of our form as we went into the classroom. I had to decide which ones I'd ask about husbands for Auntie. There were some whose relatives you definitely wouldn't want swimming in your gene pool. That was one of the reasons why I wasn't asking George Botley.

'Hurry up, Eight A.' Mr Arora swept through the classroom door like a whirlwind, his arms full, dropping books and folders as he went. He was looking pale and tetchy, as all the teachers were, and he was getting paler and tetchier every day as the inspectors' visit approached. 'I expected you all to be sitting down five minutes ago. Get your books out. Who left that chewing gum on the bookcase?'

We all rushed smartly to our seats, even people like

Darren Bell who thought they were hard (and actually *were* hard). In the mood Sleeping Beauty was in, you could get sent straight to Mr Grimwade for putting a foot wrong. And the mood Mr Grimwade was in, you could end up painting the outside of the school or repairing the roof.

Mr Arora chucked his books and files down on the desk and grimly attacked the register. 'George Botley.'

'Here, sir,' Botley called. He followed up with a loud burp which made the low-lifes in the class snigger.

'Ambajit Dhillon.'

'Here, sir,' I called. And then, absolutely from nowhere, I got this blinding idea.

The solution to our problem was sitting straight in front of me.

I grabbed my rough book and scrawled, *'Mr Arora!'* on a clean page. Then I pushed it across to Kim.

She looked at it blankly and wrote, *'What about him?'*

'I've found Auntie a husband,' I scribbled triumphantly. *'Mr Arora! What do you think?'*

Kim looked nervous. *'I think I'm having a panic attack.'*

'Line up for assembly, please,' Mr Arora called as the bell rang. 'And Botley, don't stand behind Amina Khosla. It took us ten minutes to untie her plaits yesterday morning.'

'You're not serious?' Kim gasped, as we put our books away. 'Mr *Arora*?'

'Why not?' I replied. 'He's perfect in every way.'

'But you don't know if he's married already,' Kim said. 'And there's no way you can possibly find out.'

I was amused. 'That's what you think.' I went over to Mr Arora, who was standing by the door on Botleywatch. 'Sir, can I ask you something?'

Mr Arora nodded. 'Of course, Amber.'

'Are you married, sir?' So it was a bit cheeky, but I reckoned I was enough of a favourite to get away with it.

Mr Arora's handsome face crinkled into a smile. 'No, I'm not, Amber,' he replied. 'Why? Are you offering?'

The rest of the class sniggered and I blushed daintily. George Botley even looked jealous, the fool.

'I'd never have had the nerve to do that,' Kim said weakly as I joined her at the back of the line. 'I'd have dropped down dead. I'd have shrivelled up and died. I'd have—'

'Yes, well,' I said victoriously. 'Now we know.'

'Mr *Arora*?' Geena shrieked. 'You've got to be joking!'

'Why?' I asked. Jazz was pulling faces too. I'd rushed to tell them my idea at break time, and this was the annoying result.

'Because he's *gorgeous*, that's why,' Geena groaned. 'He's a boy babe. He's much too good for Auntie.'

'Anyway, isn't he younger than she is?' Jazz asked.

I scowled. 'Only a couple of years, I think.'

'He'd never fancy her,' Geena scoffed.

'Why not?' I argued.

'I suppose she *is* quite pretty,' Jazz said grudgingly.

'Whoever marries Auntie is going to be our uncle,' I reminded them. 'Do you really want someone with a wooden leg or a sad specimen who collects bus tickets?'

Geena nodded. 'That's true.'

'Can you imagine how jealous all the girls would be if Mr Arora was our uncle?' Jazz added, beginning to warm to the idea. 'We could sell photos of him and locks of his hair and stuff.'

Geena and I did not reply.

'Oh, all right,' Jazz muttered. 'It was just an *idea*.'

'Right,' I said. 'We're going to have to do our best to get them together.'

'And how exactly are we going to do that?' Jazz asked.

Geena looked encouragingly at me. 'Yes, Amber, how?'

That was a question all right. I had absolutely no idea. 'Why do you always expect *me* to come up with all the answers?' I blustered.

Jazz turned to Geena. 'She's got absolutely no idea,' she said in disgust.

'Oh, really, Amber!' Geena snapped. 'You'll have to do better than this.'

I gritted my teeth. 'When's the next parents' evening?'

'When we get our reports,' Jazz replied.

That was at least five months away. Five months of Auntie interfering and making us cook and stopping Dad from buying us stuff and sending us to bed early. No human being alive could be expected to put up with that.

'All right,' I muttered. 'I'll think about it.' I eyeballed my sisters sternly. 'We'll *all* think about it. There must be a way.'

Brave words. They haunted me for the rest of the day. It was all I could think of. Luckily, we had the student, Miss Véronique, for double French after break, and she was too busy trying to stop George Botley looking up rude words in the dictionary to notice that I didn't do much work. At lunch time I met Geena and Jazz in the drama studio to paint backdrops for the special assembly. Geena's best idea was this: we wait until Mr Arora is on break duty, then Geena pretends to be ill and faints. A phone call brings Auntie rushing to the school, and she and Mr Arora meet for the first time.

I accused Geena of hoping that Mr Arora would pick her up and carry her in his strong arms to the school office. Geena said, what was wrong with that? I then added that it was a much better idea if *I* fainted, as I was in his class and had plenty of time to choose my moment. But Geena was hovering menacingly over me with a paintbrush, so I decided to let her have her way – this time.

Nothing had come to me by the end of the day, but I wasn't giving up. Not when we walked out of school at four o'clock and saw Dad waiting outside in the car.

'Look, your dad's here,' said Kim, the queen of stating the obvious. She was trailing along with us, determined not to be left behind.

Geena looked twitchy. 'Why? What for?'

'It'll be something to do with Hitler in a sari,' I muttered. 'You can bet your bottom dollar.'

'I can't cope with Dad turning up unexpectedly all the time,' Jazz said in an agitated voice. 'I'm not used to it.'

Dad was fidgeting in the driver's seat. He looked massively uncomfortable. 'Hi, girls,' he said awkwardly. We looked at him with raised eyebrows and he cleared his throat. 'Er – your auntie called me at work and asked me to pick you up,' he stammered. 'She wants us to have a nice family dinner tonight.'

Geena snorted in disgust. 'Dad, do you actually *like* her interfering all the time?' she demanded, a bit recklessly.

Dad tried to look stern and failed badly. 'She's just trying to help, that's all,' he said lamely. 'Oh, and you're to bring any of your friends who want to come.'

Geena, Jazz and I immediately glanced over our shoulders to check that none of our mates had over-heard.

'Thanks, I'd love to,' Kim said in a pleased voice.

'No,' I said. 'You don't want to do that.'

'Oh, I do,' Kim assured me.

'Kim.' I said her name so savagely, every letter was one beat long. 'You don't *really* want to come, *do you*?'

'Yes, please,' Kim said cheerfully.

'I'll talk to you later,' I said under my breath as we got into the car.

Kim sagged, looking a bit worried, but it didn't stop her getting in too.

As Dad drove home, I daydreamed in the back of the car. A wedding. Auntie in red and gold with rows of tinkling bangles on her wrists, hands patterned with henna. Mr Arora in a white suit and a dashing pink turban. Singing and dancing and feasting. And then the bride leaves home and I get my bedroom back and everything goes on exactly as it did before she arrived . . .

'What happened to Ma Macey?' Geena asked, as we drew up outside our house.

We peered out of the car windows. There was a trowel, some clippers, a pair of gardening gloves and a black bag half full of weeds in her front garden. But there was no sign of the other old bag.

'Maybe the paperboy murdered her and buried her in her own front garden,' I suggested.

'She'll probably rise again and haunt us for ever,' Jazz added. She put her hands out in front of her and intoned in a zombie-like voice, *'Why don't you all go back to where you came from?'*

'Girls,' Dad said half-heartedly.

Geena unlocked the front door. We heard voices as she swung it open.

'No,' Geena whispered, her eyes out on stalks. 'Not even Auntie would go that far.'

'She wouldn't,' I breathed.

But she would and she had. There was Auntie in the kitchen, holding the kettle and smiling a cheerful welcome. And there, perched on a chair and looking as uncomfortable as if she was sitting on a spike, was Mrs Macey.

Jazz made a kind of shocked gurgling noise. Geena and I stared. Dad looked stunned.

'Hello, everyone,' Auntie said casually. 'How was school? Gloria's just popped in for a cup of coffee.'

Gloria? Oh no. This would never do.

Mrs Macey shuffled around in her seat. She couldn't quite meet my eyes, and I guessed that she was remembering the last time we'd met.

'And who's this?' Auntie turned to Kim.

'This is Kim,' I told the traitor crossly. How dare she invite Mrs Macey into *our* house?

'Hello, Kim,' Auntie said. 'Would you like a cup of coffee? You're quite safe, it's Nescafé.' She turned to smile at Mrs Macey. 'Gloria thought I was going to poison her with some strange brand of Indian coffee.'

Mrs Macey looked positively on fire with embarrassment. She cleared her throat. 'I must be going,' she muttered. 'Thank you for the coffee – er – Susie.'

'Any time,' Auntie said with a wave of her hand.

'I'll see you out,' Dad added.

Mrs Macey did her best not to look amazed that Indian men could have good manners. Mumbling goodbyes, she scuttled from the kitchen towards the front door.

I consulted Geena with a glance, my eyebrows raised. She nodded. Auntie had come from India. She didn't know that sometimes things could be difficult here. It was time she was told.

'You know Mrs Macey doesn't like us, Auntie,' Geena said pointedly.

'Yes,' Auntie agreed, filling the kettle. 'That's why I invited her. I thought it was time we got to know each other.'

I cast up my eyes. 'She doesn't like us because we're Indian,' I said.

'I know,' Auntie replied calmly.

'You *know*?' Jazz roared.

'So why are you being nice to her?' I demanded.

Auntie shrugged. 'Because now Mrs Macey feels bad for not liking us when we've been good to her.' She smiled. 'Maybe now she'll change her mind.'

'Oh no, I don't think so,' Geena said icily. 'Mrs

Macey will just turn into one of those people who says, *Well, I don't like Pakis, but you're all right because I know you.*'

'Yes,' said Auntie thoughtfully. 'But if she doesn't hate all of us, at least it's a start.'

I remembered Mrs Macey muttering that we were 'all the same', and I wondered if Auntie was right. Just in time, I caught myself. Eek. For a minute there I'd nearly given Auntie some *credit*. Scary.

'I think that's a good idea,' Kim said.

As one we turned to stare at her. Kim didn't voice opinions. She didn't *have* opinions. Or she'd never had them before, at least.

'Good.' Auntie smiled at her. 'Kim, you come and help me make the pizzas, and we'll have a little chat. Amber, Geena and Jazz can lay the table.'

I didn't like leaving Kim alone with Auntie, but I didn't have any choice. Every time I went into the kitchen to collect cutlery or plates or salad dressing, Kim and Auntie had their heads together over the pizza bases. One time they were laughing uproariously. Another time they were talking about Kim's mum. And once they were talking in lowered voices and I couldn't hear what they were saying. I began to feel seriously uneasy.

Dad was hanging around the living room, getting in our way as we laid the table. He looked jittery and jumpy, as if he'd rather be a million miles away. He'd spent more time in the house over the last few weeks than he'd done for the whole year since Mum. I wondered what Auntie had been saying to him. Had she been nagging him the way she nagged us? Was he getting as fed up with her as we were? I really hoped so.

The pizzas were made, and they smelled delicious. I had to give it to Auntie: she was a great cook. We all gathered round the table, mouths watering.

'Save the piece with the burned cheese for me,' I ordered. 'I like it like that.'

I went back into the kitchen to collect the last pizza. Auntie was just lifting it out of the oven. She slid it onto a plate and turned to face me.

'Tell me, Amber,' she said softly. 'Why is Kim so unhappy?'

My jaw dropped. Of all the things she could have said, I wasn't expecting that. 'She's not unhappy,' I said. *Here she goes again, interfering in something she knows nothing about.* 'She's just – Kim.'

'You should speak to her.' Auntie glanced sideways at me to test my reaction. 'If people are unhappy about something, it's better to talk about things than hide them away inside.'

No one could ever accuse her of being subtle. Well, I could walk all over someone else's feelings too, no problem.

'Why didn't my mother like you?' I asked abruptly.

She wasn't expecting *that*. Her face changed and her eyes dropped. For once, I'd completely floored her.

'Here.' She held out the plate to me, visibly pulling herself together. 'Just remember what I've said, won't you?'

'Not if I can help it,' I said under my breath as I walked out. Didn't she realize that the only thing we were unhappy about was *her*?

We might have ended up murdering Auntie and burying her in *our* back garden if I hadn't had my next brilliant idea. Everything fell into place the next morning. We were in class waiting for Mr Arora to arrive for registration.

'So, Kim,' I said for the eighth time. 'What were you and Auntie talking about in the kitchen last night?'

Kim's eyes became vague. 'Oh, just stuff,' she said feebly, for the eighth time. I gave up and turned my back on her to talk to Chelsea and Sharelle. They were perched on our table, giggling.

'Who did *that*?' I moaned, as a loud, riproaring raspberry sounded around the classroom.

'It's Botley,' said Sharelle. 'He's got one of those remote control fart machines hidden in his bag.'

'Oh, God,' I said. 'How original.'

Mr Arora swept into the room, eyes darting here and there. I wondered if Botley would be stupid enough to use the machine during registration. I don't know why I even wondered. At the exact moment Mr Arora's bottom made contact with his chair, a loud noise reverberated around the room. No one dared to laugh.

'Botley,' said Mr Arora in a dangerous voice, 'bring that thing to me immediately.'

'How did you know it was me, sir?' George asked foolishly.

'Just a wild guess,' Mr Arora snapped.

'I was only trying to cheer everyone up, sir,' George protested, shambling out to the front of the class with the machine in his hand. 'You know, with the inspectors coming next week and everything.'

Mr Arora's left eye twitched maniacally. 'You will report to Mr Grimwade tonight, Botley,' he said through gritted teeth. 'And he will give you a letter to take home to your mother. She will be invited to visit the school so that we can discuss your consistently annoying behaviour. Is that clear?'

Yes. It was clear. It was so obvious.

CHAPTER 7

'Oh no,' Geena moaned. She put her hands over her ears. 'I'm going to pretend you didn't say that.'

'But it's a fantastic idea,' I protested.

'It's a stupid idea,' Jazz said. 'It's the most stupid idea you've ever had, Amber. You must be brain-dead.'

'Oh, don't be shy,' I said. 'Tell me what you really think, why don't you.'

'Let's get this straight.' Geena shifted a pot of gold paint out of the way, and we climbed onto the stage. We were in the drama studio at break time, pretending to be painting the assembly backdrops. I'd suggested meeting there because it was quiet and we wouldn't be overheard. Ms Woods always dashed off to the staff room at the first ring of the bell to get her caffeine shot, so there was no one around. 'You're going to start behaving badly so that Mr Arora gets fed up and wants Dad to come up to the school and sort it out.'

'Now I'm *definitely* having a panic attack,' Kim groaned. Her face did look white. She'd tailed me along the corridors as usual, even though I'd tried to give her the slip.

'Well, don't breathe too deeply,' I said. 'There's a lot of paint fumes round here.' I turned back to Geena and Jazz. 'You know what Auntie's like. She'll want to come too and stick her nose in. She and Mr Arora get together. Perfect. I can see it all now. Eyes meeting across an empty classroom . . .'

'Aren't you forgetting one tiny, tiny detail?' Geena asked.

'What?'

Geena made a megaphone with her hands around her mouth. 'You'll get into trouble, idiot!' she yelled.

'I know that,' I said, just managing to keep my dignity under this barrage of insults. 'I think it's worth it to get rid of her.'

'Yes, but—' Jazz began.

'What?'

'Nothing.' Jazz looked embarrassed. That doesn't come easily to her, so it had to be something important.

'Oh, go on,' I said. 'It's your turn to insult me. Geena's had her say.'

'I haven't finished yet,' Geena warned. 'I'm just taking a breather.'

Jazz didn't look at us. She was carefully drawing circles with her toe on the floor of the stage.

'We-ll,' she mumbled, 'I was just thinking. We're kind of, you know, doing all right at the moment. After – after—'

'Yes,' Geena said quickly.

After what happened with Mum, she meant. I swallowed. The pain, when I allowed it to come, was still raw, and the depth of it took me unawares. It left me breathless and hurting as if I'd been punched hard and low.

Jazz was still trying to explain what she wanted to say without actually saying it. 'And everyone thinks we're doing fine and that we're cool and this could sort of – sort of—'

'We get it,' I broke in.

What Jazz meant was that this would ruin the life we'd carefully constructed for ourselves over the last year. It would put paid to the belief that the Dhillon girls were coping, and even doing better than that. They were getting on with their lives, bravely and confidently. The three of us had never got together and decided to do this in so many words. We'd just bonded together as a perfect unit, and this was how it had happened. Silently we'd all followed the same lead, although I don't think any of us could have said whose idea it was.

I felt uneasy. Our performance for the outside world had kept us going for over a year. I didn't know what would happen if I started to mess with the image we'd created for ourselves. But if meant getting rid of Auntie, maybe it was worth the risk.

'Look,' I said, 'it won't be that bad. Arora and Grimwade aren't going to hang around, not with the inspectors coming. They'll get Dad and Auntie up

the school as soon as possible. It'll be quick and pain-
less.'

Kim whimpered like a sick kitten. I grinned at her.

'Don't worry,' I said. 'I don't expect you to help
me.'

'I would if you wanted me to,' said Kim weakly.

I felt one of the sudden rushes of affection I sometimes have for Kim. 'You'd die if you got a detention,'
I said, patting her on the back.

'What exactly would you do?' Jazz asked. 'Smoke
in the loos? Snog boys behind the bike sheds? Play
truant?'

'I certainly hope you're not going to start smoking,'
Geena said. 'Dad would have a fit. Anyway, you
wouldn't like the taste.'

I glanced sideways at her. 'How would you know?'

'I tried it once,' Geena said dismissively. 'It's over-
rated.'

I stored the information up as possible blackmail
later. 'I wasn't planning on going that far,' I replied. 'I
was thinking of something more along the lines of
George Botley. I've already got a few ideas.'

Geena looked sober. 'So you're really going to do
it.'

I nodded.

'Well, we can't stop you,' Geena said. 'But be
careful.'

'Yes, be careful,' Jazz echoed anxiously.

'I will.'

I meant it. I did. I was planning to be careful. I was *scared*. This was a big step for me after the last year. It would be like going from prom queen to school geek. From being someone everyone envied to being someone like *George Botley*. I was going to be the Georgina Botley of Class 8A. It wasn't a nice thought.

Being perfect hadn't been easy. But I'd been that way for so long, I'd forgotten how to annoy teachers. I sat in my maths class with Mr Arora after break and wondered what I should do. If you can believe it, my mind was a blank. I could think of nothing. Should I begin with something big that would disrupt the whole class, or should I start small and work my way up? I didn't know.

I was sitting next to Sharelle, and Kim was to the side of me. She kept darting nervous glances across the gap, as if she expected me to spontaneously combust at any moment. I felt nervous enough, and she was putting me off.

'Go on,' I muttered to myself, twirling my ruler in an agitated manner. Mr Arora was patrolling the classroom, marking books over people's shoulders. I could stick out my foot and trip him up. I could throw my maths book at him. I could pinch his bottom . . .

Mr Arora walked past me. I didn't do anything and I could have kicked myself.

'Do something bad,' I whispered. 'Something. *Anything.*'

'Amber!' Sharelle moaned. I was so preoccupied, I'd accidentally stuck my ruler in her ear. I apologized.

'What's the matter with you?' she grumbled. 'You've been acting strange all morning.' She stared speculatively at me through narrowed eyes. 'That's how my Uncle Mac started. Talking to himself.'

'Well, shoot me if I start collecting bus tickets,' I said, bending my head over my book.

'Amber –' Mr Arora had doubled back around the classroom and was at my side again as I wrote in the last answer – 'have you finished?'

'Yes, sir,' I said.

I watched as he marked my algebra. Everything, including the most difficult sums, was correct. I hadn't even had the wit to do them all wrong. I was disgusted with myself.

'Excellent, as usual, Amber,' said Mr Arora in his gentle voice. 'Go on to page forty-two.'

I looked up at him. There's no doubt that Mr Arora is gorgeous, but if he's got one *tiny* fault, it's his ears. They stick out ever so slightly. He wears his hair long to cover them up a bit, but they're definitely there, just peeking through.

'All right,' I said, 'Big Ears.'

At least, I *thought* I said it. But I could only have said it in my head, because Mr Arora didn't turn white. The class didn't gasp. Kim didn't faint. And now I'd lost my chance. Mr Arora was turning away from me. *Do it.*

'Oi, Big Ears,' I croaked. But my voice wouldn't come out properly.

Mr Arora turned back, looking puzzled. 'Did you say something, Amber?'

Everyone in the classroom was staring at me. I could see Kim clutching the edge of the table, her knuckles bloodless. I collapsed like a house of cards.

'Er – I can't remember, sir,' I mumbled.

'It sounded like Britney Spears to me,' Sharelle said helpfully. I would have liked to kill her on the spot. It would have been one way of getting Auntie and Dad called up the school.

I spent the last ten minutes of the lesson giving myself a good talking to. By the time the bell rang, I'd psyched myself up to go for it next lesson. Netball with Miss Thomas.

'*Not* Thomas the Tank Engine,' Kim moaned, as we changed into our kit. 'She'll murder you, Amber.'

Kim was not exaggerating for once. I gulped. Now I was *really* scared.

'Look at the weather,' Chelsea complained, staring out of the changing-room windows. The wind was howling and screeching around the building, and the trees were being tossed from side to side and bent double. 'Only a lunatic like Thomas could expect us to play netball on a day like this.'

'I heard that, Chelsea Dixon,' thundered Miss Thomas, appearing as if by magic in the changing-room doorway. 'Detention at lunch time. Write out one hundred times, *I must not question my teachers' decisions or call them lunatics.*'

'I wish I'd said that,' I remarked to Kim. 'Then *I'd* be in detention.'

Kim did not reply. Possibly her throat had closed up through blind fear.

We trailed reluctantly out of the changing rooms into the gale which was blowing straight into our faces. We did prize-winning impressions of acute angles and it took us five minutes to get to the netball courts instead of the usual thirty seconds. I spent the time thinking up things I could say which would get me a detention. Sometimes a simple 'Hello, miss' was enough to get Thomas riled.

As it turned out, it was all for nothing. I would have needed a loudhailer to say anything to Miss Thomas which she could actually hear. The wind whipped all the words from our mouths and tore them away, making conversation impossible. Netball, too. Passing the ball was out of the question. At last Thomas let us scuttle back inside, but only after a litter bin had bowled across the court and nearly knocked Kim over.

'I'm hopeless,' I complained, as we changed. 'Useless.' I glanced at the clock. The hands were ticking round to lunch time. 'I'm going to have to tell Geena and Jazz that I'm not getting anywhere. They'll only say I told you so.'

'Let's go to lunch,' Kim said. 'I'll buy you your favourite treacle pudding.'

'Thanks, but I can't.' I buttoned my shirt. 'I've got an assembly rehearsal first.'

'Oh.' Kim looked disappointed.

I was still getting changed when the bell rang. By the time I got to the drama studio, most of the rest of the assembly cast were there, including Geena and Jazz. Ms Woods didn't notice I was late because she was arguing with Kyra Hollins. They'd had this row three times already. Kyra, who was one of Geena's mates, had an aunt who knew someone who was a Buddhist. So she'd been forced into taking part in the assembly by Ms Woods.

'Miss, I keep telling you, *I'm* not a Buddhist,' Kyra complained. 'My auntie just knows someone who is.'

'And as I told you before, Kyra,' Ms Woods snapped, her hair looking bigger and wilder than ever, 'I'm not interested.'

Geena nudged me. 'We've got something to tell you, Jazz and I,' she whispered.

I glanced at her. Geena's eyes were shining and she looked excited. Jazz beamed at me and nodded. I began, for some reason, to feel slightly uneasy.

'The other kids in my class keep taking the mick out of me,' Kyra said sullenly.

'Kyra,' said Ms Woods through clenched teeth, 'I am a Buddhist myself and it is a wonderful religion. It is a religion of peace and tranquillity and calm acceptance. Now shut up before I give you a detention. Where are my Christians?'

115

We all moved into position at the sides of the stage. Geena, Jazz and I had learned our words already, but some of the others were looking dazed and clutching bits of paper. Daniel Cohen, for instance, was sweet but as thick as two very short, thick planks. Even if he wrote his words out on his hand, he wouldn't be able to *read* them. However, as there weren't many Jewish kids in the school, he'd been forced into taking part.

Ms Woods was struggling with the backdrops. Instead of the map of the world showing the spread of the major religions, we were standing in front of Widow Twankey's kitchen from last year's lower school panto, *Aladdin*. I hoped the inspectors had a sense of humour.

'What have you got to tell me, then?' I asked Geena in a low voice.

She smiled. 'Jazz and I are going to help you,' she said.

'Help me?'

'Yes,' Jazz chimed in. 'We're going to behave badly too. We're *all* going to behave badly.'

'What?' I was outraged. 'That's ridiculous.'

'Why?' they said together.

'Because—' I stopped to work out why. 'Why should we *all* get into trouble?'

'We always stick together, don't we?' Geena said.

'Yes, all for one and one for all,' Jazz agreed.

'That's so not true,' I said. 'What about the time I

116

accidentally broke Dad's laptop and then pretended it had been nicked? You and Jazz found it and dropped me right in it.'

'Oh, that.' Geena waved her hand dismissively. 'I was just trying to get in with Dad because I wanted a new CD player.'

'And I just wanted to get you into trouble,' Jazz added. 'But this is different.'

'If we all start messing about, Grimwade will get Dad and Auntie up the school a lot quicker,' Geena said sensibly.

I wanted to argue. I couldn't. I knew they were right. I just didn't want them in on my idea.

'You can't stop us, Amber,' Geena pointed out. 'Anyway, I've already started.'

'You've *started*?' I felt almost suffocated by jealousy. 'You've started? How? When?'

'I dropped my German book on the floor on purpose,' Geena said proudly. 'Twice.'

'Good one,' I said. 'I bet Grimwade's dashing off a furious letter to Dad as we speak.'

Geena looked cross. 'You're not funny, Amber, and you're certainly not clever.'

'What did Miss Berger do?' Jazz asked.

'She didn't, actually, notice,' Geena admitted. 'But I've got some other tricks up my sleeve.'

'Ooh, I'm going to think of something naughty to do this afternoon,' Jazz said eagerly.

Ms Woods had finally got the right backdrop into

position. 'Right, Christians and Sikhs stand by,' she panted.

We stepped out onto the stage. The uneasy feeling I'd had was intensified. Now the stakes were higher. We were playing a dangerous game. It was a game we had to win.

'Amber?' Sharelle poked me in the ribs. 'Why are you staring at Botley?'

Because I'd decided that there was only one thing to do. If I was going to be annoying, and more annoying than Geena and Jazz, I would have to study a master of the art. And there was nobody more supreme at winding up teachers than George Botley.

'She fancies him.' Chelsea snorted with laughter.

'Oh, sure,' I said. 'Do I look mentally defective?'

George had strolled into the classroom after lunch with an open can of Coke. While we were waiting for Mr Arora to arrive to take the register, he was amusing himself by filling his mouth with liquid and squirting it at people. He hadn't dared squirt any at me yet, but I could tell from the glint in his eye that he was thinking about it. Kim had escaped too, by getting the biggest book in the classroom, a world atlas, and propping it up on her table to form a shield.

'Can you imagine a date with Botley?' Sharelle mused. 'He'd probably take you to detention, seeing as he spends most of his time there.'

'Imagine snogging him.' Chelsea shuddered. 'It'd be like kissing a dead animal.' She shrieked loudly as a stream of Coke flashed past her ear. 'Botley, you're dead!'

'Let me, Chelsea,' I said.

A little devil had jumped onto my shoulder. Hardly registering what I was doing, I plunged forward, grabbed the can of Coke and poured it over George's head.

The first thing that struck me was just how much a can of soft drink holds. The brown fizzy liquid streamed out, soaking George's hair, then his face, then his clothes in the space of seconds.

Everyone was too shocked to say a word, including George, including me. At that very moment Mr Arora walked in. His eyes almost fell out of his head.

'George Botley.'

George turned to face him. He peered through rivulets of Coke running down his face, his trainers squelching. 'Yes, sir?'

Mr Arora advanced menacingly. 'Would you care to tell me what you're doing?'

The atmosphere in the classroom was tense. Kim was hiding behind the atlas, and Chelsea, Sharelle and the rest of the class were goggling at me. No one could believe what they'd seen with their own eyes.

'I'm all wet, sir,' George muttered.

'Yes, I can see that,' Mr Arora agreed. His gaze flicked to the empty can which I'd put down on

George's table. 'And the reason why is . . . ?'

Everyone looked at me. I felt nervous but exhilarated. This was a bit wilder than dropping a German book on the floor (twice). I was sure to get into trouble. I waited.

'I tipped a can of Coke over myself, sir,' George said feebly.

There was a collective intake of breath from the whole class. Now it was my turn to goggle at *him*. What was he doing, the fool?

'Sir—' I began.

Mr Arora ignored me. 'Why?' he enquired in the kind of pleasant voice that can only mean tremendous trouble two minutes later.

'I thought it would be a laugh,' George replied.

'And was it?' Mr Arora asked, still pleasant.

'Sort of,' George muttered, wiping Coke out of his eyes.

'*Sir*—' I began again, waving my hand in the air. I heard Kim moan faintly behind her atlas.

But Mr Arora continued to ignore me. 'Go to Lost Property and find yourself some dry clothes, Botley,' he said through gritted teeth. 'And then bring a mop from the cleaner's cupboard. When you return, we shall spend a good deal of time discussing exactly how many detentions you are going to be attending for the next – oh – several weeks—'

'Sir, it was me,' I broke in, unable to stand it any longer. 'I tipped the Coke over George.'

'No, she didn't,' George said gallantly.

I could have hit him over the head with the empty can. 'I *did*, sir.'

Mr Arora looked at me as if I was mad. He went over to his table and opened the register, and the class hurried to their seats in a state of high excitement. Meanwhile, George squelched over to the door, giving me a knowing wink which made me want to slap him.

'God, that was amazing,' Sharelle said, staring at me so hard I thought her eyeballs were going to pop out. 'I can't believe you did that.'

'Wasn't it sweet the way Georgie took the blame?' Chelsea crowed. 'I always knew he fancied you, Amber.'

'Oh, be quiet,' I snapped. 'Can't one of you go and tell Arora that it was me? He'd believe you.'

Chelsea and Sharelle also looked at me as if I was mad. Muttering to myself, I stomped over to my seat. I'd screwed up my courage to do something bad and nobody really appreciated it. It was sickening.

The afternoon did get worse. George Botley returned from Lost Property wearing a shirt that was too big and trousers that were too short and flapped around his ankles like flags. He kept winking and smiling at me all through afternoon classes. I was terrified that he was going to corner me at home time and demand something in return for his silence, like – oh, horror – a date. So when the bell rang at the end of the day I made a run for it and hid behind the bike sheds until Geena and Jazz came out.

'What's all this about you and George Botley?' Geena demanded immediately. She sounded just a shade envious.

'Yeah, it's all round the school that you tipped Coca-Cola over him and then shoved the empty can down his trousers,' Jazz added.

'Someone said that when Mr Arora tried to tell you off, you punched him on the nose,' Geena went on. 'But I don't believe that for a minute.'

'You didn't, did you, Amber?' Jazz asked eagerly.

'Don't get over-excited,' I said. 'I did tip Coke over Botley, but he told Mr Arora that he did it himself. God knows why.'

Geena and Jazz began to snigger. 'Oh, I think *we* know why,' Jazz chortled.

'Look, can we get back to the really important thing here?' I snapped, as I hurried them off down the road. I didn't know where Kim was. Didn't care, either. And luckily Botley was nowhere to be seen. 'Did either of you manage to annoy a teacher this afternoon?'

'I sort of did,' Jazz said. 'Miss Véronique brought in loads of food so we could practise shopping in French, and I ate half the baguette when she wasn't looking.'

'Was she cross?' Geena asked.

Jazz nodded. 'A bit. But she said it was past its best before date. She'd got it half price from Mr Attwal.'

'What about you?' I asked Geena.

'I left all my books for this afternoon's lessons behind *on purpose*,' Geena said proudly. 'Left them in our classroom, just like that.'

'Is that all?' I was not impressed. 'We're complete *amateurs*.'

We walked on in silence. I didn't like to admit it, but my plan wasn't working. We were weak and feeble when it came to being bad. And all the time, Auntie was still going about her annoying business, doing her best to make our lives miserable and succeeding.

'It's hopeless, isn't it?' Geena said, as we walked up to Mr Attwal's shop. 'Maybe we're just too nice.'

'George Botley thinks Amber's *nice*,' Jazz said wickedly.

'Give that up right now,' I said, twisting her ear, 'or suffer the consequences.'

Mr Attwal was sitting in the shop window, his head bent over a pile of textbooks. We waved as we went by, but he didn't look up.

'What we need,' I said, thinking aloud, 'is something to get us *started*. Something that makes everyone sit up and take notice.'

'AARGH!' Jazz roared.

Something – someone – had just swept past us and tugged the pink scrunchie from her ponytail. It was our old enemy, the paperboy. Laughing, he pedalled off down our street, waving the scrunchie over his head like a trophy.

'You give that back!' Jazz yelled.

'After him,' I shouted.

We gave chase. We didn't have a hope of catching him and we knew it, even though he stopped to hurl the evening paper first over our gate and then over Mrs Macey's. But then, as he swung his bike round, the wheels slipped. The bike slid over on its side, and the paperboy went sprawling onto the road. The two bags spilled newspapers and magazines in crumpled heaps.

'Get him!' Geena shouted triumphantly like a policeman on TV. The three of us raced up the street like hounds after a fox.

I don't know what we were going to do when we got him, but we didn't even have a chance to think about it. As we skidded to a halt and loomed over the fallen paperboy like the three witches in *Macbeth*, our front gate opened. Auntie came out with a trowel in her hand. She was wearing old jeans and a loose white shirt which I recognized as an old one of Dad's. Her hair was tied up on top of her head. She looked annoyingly glamorous for someone weeding a garden.

'Leo?' Her eyebrows went up when she saw the paperboy sitting on the tarmac. 'Are you all right?'

I might have known she'd be on first-name terms with him by now.

'I think so,' the paperboy – sorry, *Leo* – mumbled. He clutched his knee. His combat trousers had ripped, and there was a faint seep of blood through the hole.

'He stole my scrunchie!' Jazz howled.

Auntie picked it up from the road without comment and passed it to her. 'I think you'd better come inside, Leo,' she said, helping him up. 'You look a bit shaken. The girls will pick up the papers.'

'Oh, we will, will we?' Geena muttered.

'Maybe if *Leo* stopped and got off his bike and put the newspapers through the letter boxes once in a while, he wouldn't have accidents,' I remarked under my breath.

Auntie stared at us for what seemed a very long time. 'Leo's in a hurry because he does two paper rounds every morning and every evening,' she said at last. 'Do you know why?'

'No,' I mumbled. I had a feeling I wasn't going to enjoy the answer.

'His brother's ill, and the family are saving up to take him to America for an operation,' Auntie said crisply. 'All of Leo's earnings from his paper rounds go towards the fund.' She led him over to the gate. 'It's amazing what you can learn from people just by bothering to talk to them once in a while,' she said over her shoulder. She turned from us to Leo. 'Come inside – I'll make you a cup of tea.'

'Thanks, Auntie,' Leo said gratefully.

They went into the house, leaving us all feeling less than a centimetre tall.

'Well, how were we supposed to know?' Geena said, quite reasonably, but it didn't make us feel any better.

We picked up the newspapers and put them back into the bags. As we carried them up the garden path, Auntie popped her head round the front door.

'Leo's not feeling up to finishing his rounds today,' she said. 'So I said you girls would do them. It's very easy. The addresses are written on the papers. Oh, and don't be too long because you've got all your homework to do.' Then she popped back inside like an evil jack-in-the-box.

Geena said a very rude word. 'That is *it*. I can't put up with her for a minute longer.' She dropped the heavy bag of newspapers on the path and kicked it.

I, however, had a gleam in my eye. 'Homework,' I said slowly. I unzipped my Nike bag and took out the maths worksheet Mr Arora had given us. I tore it neatly into eight pieces and tossed them into the black bin.

'I hope that wasn't anything important,' Geena remarked, watching me.

'Oh, it was,' I said. 'Very important. My maths homework.'

Geena grinned. 'Oh, I *get* it,' she said. She sorted through her bag and pulled out a notebook. She ripped three pages out, scrumpled them into a ball and added them to the bin. 'Goodbye, environmental studies homework.'

Jazz's eyes were out on stalks. 'What are you *doing*?'

'You know I said we needed something to get us started?' I threw my science worksheets in the bin, followed by some French vocabulary. 'This is it.'

CHAPTER 8

'This just isn't like you, Amber.' Mr Arora tapped his fingers on the table in an agitated manner. 'This is the second day you haven't handed in any homework. I've had complaints from . . .' He flipped open his notebook. 'Miss Patel, Mrs Kirke, Mrs Murray, Mr Lucas, Miss Jackson and Mr Khan.'

'I think you'll find you've missed out Mrs Parker and Mr Hernandez,' I said. '*Sir*.' It was shocking how easy it was to be cheeky once you'd actually got off to a start.

But unluckily, Mr Arora didn't seem annoyed. He stared at me quizzically as if he couldn't quite decide what to do next.

'And it isn't just the homework, either,' he said at last. 'Miss Patel has told me that you talked all through her lesson and then walked out before the bell rang.'

'The lesson was boring, sir,' I said.

Suddenly we'd got it all going on. In just two days, Geena, Jazz and I had the teachers flapping about like headless chickens, wondering what was happening.

It surely couldn't be long before they gave Dad a call. But I wished Mr Arora would stop looking at me with that concerned expression on his face. I wanted him to be mad. I wanted him to yell and shout and give me detentions.

'I'm hearing the same kind of things about Geena and Jasvinder,' Mr Arora went on. 'What's happening?'

I stood there silently.

'Is something troubling you, Amber?' he asked gently. 'Is there anything you want to tell me?'

'Only one thing, sir,' I said. 'I won't be doing that geometry homework you gave us.'

Mr Arora sighed deeply. 'I'd like you to reconsider that decision, Amber,' he said. 'In fact, I'd like you to go home and think about your behaviour over the last few days. Then I want you to come and discuss it with me before the inspectors arrive next week. All right?'

'*Discuss* it?' I repeated incredulously.

Mr Arora nodded at me and gathered up his papers. Disgruntled, I grabbed my bag and flounced out of the classroom. What was the matter with teachers today? They weren't half strict enough. I didn't want talk. I wanted action.

It was the end of the day, and the school had emptied about ten minutes ago. I strolled down the echoing corridors, singing a Bollywood tune to myself. I felt good. I didn't know why, but it was an exciting feeling. I wasn't scared any more. After all, what was the worst they could do to us?

I'd told Kim not to wait for me, but Geena and Jazz were sitting on the kerb by the gate, sharing a bag of crisps. As I headed towards them, a shadow fell across my path. George Botley had sprung out from behind the wall, blocking my way.

'Hi,' he said gruffly. 'Want half my Twix?'

'No, thanks,' I said, and sidestepped him neatly. Since we'd accelerated our campaign, Botley had become ever more interested. Perhaps he thought he'd finally found his queen consort.

George looked disappointed. 'I've got a Mars bar too,' he shouted after me. His chat-up technique wasn't the greatest.

I walked as fast as I could towards Geena and Jazz without actually running. 'Let's get out of here,' I said. George was coming directly after me, a determined look on his face.

'Oh, bless,' Geena remarked. 'He's been waiting here all this time.'

'Don't start,' I snapped. 'Don't you want to know what Arora said to me?'

'I can guess,' Jazz broke in. 'He told you to go home and think about things—'

'And then come back and discuss it with him,' Geena finished.

I was amazed. 'How did you know?'

'Because that's what Mrs Kirke told me,' Geena said.

'And Mr Lucas the same,' Jazz added.

'What's going on?' I asked. 'Why are they being so nice?'

'When, in fact, we want them to scream at us and give us lots of detentions,' Geena sighed. 'It's a mystery.'

'We'll turn up the heat,' I said, glancing round to check that we'd shaken off Botley. He was skulking off home – which, thankfully, was in the opposite direction. 'Things had better get a bit wilder.'

'Oh, good.' Jazz looked pleased with herself. 'I've had a fab idea for Mr Khan's class tomorrow.'

'What?' Geena asked.

'I'm not telling you,' Jazz sniffed. 'You might *copy* me.'

'Jazz, this isn't a contest,' I said.

'No, it isn't,' Geena agreed. 'Anyway, listen to what I did today. My English teacher, Miss Davies, told us to write a story, and I wrote every word backwards. You should have seen the look on her face when I handed it in.'

'Hey, that was my idea!' I yelled. 'I *told* you I was going to do that.'

Jazz examined her fingernails. 'What were you saying about this not being a contest?' she enquired.

I elbowed her in the ribs and then the tedious round of pushing and shoving and hitting each other

131

with bags began. Geena joined in too, just for the fun of it. While I was defending myself, I thought about what had just happened. I got the feeling that Geena and Jazz were sneakily starting to enjoy themselves. Worryingly, that was how I felt. Was it a contest? Were we really trying to outdo each other? The point of all this was trying to get Auntie and Mr Arora together. Wasn't it?

We battled our way past Mr Attwal's shop. This time he saw us and waved the textbook he was reading.

'*An Idiot's Guide to Computers*,' Geena said, parrying a thrust from Jazz with her left arm. 'Well, I suppose he's got to start somewhere.'

'Truce,' I added, giving Jazz's ponytail a final pull.

'Ow.' Jazz lunged at me. But she spotted something over my shoulder that made her pull up sharply.

'Hi.' Leo was poised on his cycle in the road next to us, standing up on the pedals. We stared at him as he held out the evening paper to me.

'Er – yes,' I said helplessly, taking it. 'Thank you.'

Leo grinned and pedalled away, doing a rather spectacular wheelie.

'Watch it, Amber,' Jazz said. 'George will be getting jealous.'

'Shut up unless you want another fight,' I threatened.

'Look, Dad's home *again*,' Geena broke in. 'There's his car.'

'This is getting way out of hand,' I said, as we reached our gate.

'And there's Mrs Macey,' Jazz said agitatedly under her breath. Mrs Macey was in her front garden, putting a bag of rubbish in the dustbin. 'Are we supposed to say hello to her now or what?'

'Let's hide behind the hedge until she's gone in,' I suggested.

At that very moment, though, Mrs Macey saw us. She gave a kind of frightened half-nod and then disappeared into the house as if she'd done something extremely daring. I had the strangest sensation of a familiar world spinning suddenly out of control. Everything was different. I didn't like it.

'Hello.' Auntie was sitting in the living room with Dad's laptop on her knees. 'Had a good day at school?'

'Yes,' we all lied.

Auntie waited for us to say something else. We didn't. She sighed. 'No homework again?' Her sharp dark eyes roamed over our bags, which were about half as full as they should be. 'Is there anything I should know?'

'We told you yesterday,' I said. 'The teachers are too busy getting ready for the inspectors to give us homework.'

A loud BANG! above our heads made us instinctively duck for cover. It was followed by a faint 'Ow, that hurt.'

'Your dad's come home early to tidy up the loft,' Auntie said. 'I popped up there yesterday and I couldn't believe the mess it was in. You three could give him a hand if you haven't got any homework.'

I stared closely, suspiciously, at her. Was this one of her ruses for family togetherness? Auntie stared innocently back at me, brushing her hair from her face.

'Oh, I'm tired,' Jazz moaned. 'Can't we do it this weekend?'

'No, we're going to Inderjit's wedding,' Auntie reminded her.

Inderjit was one of our cousins. She'd been a bit wild in her day and had actually shaved her head and dated a Goth, which had gone down a storm with her parents, but now her hair had grown back again and she was having an arranged marriage. I'd forgotten it was this weekend.

'Oh, let's just do it,' Geena muttered as we trailed upstairs. 'It's easier than arguing with the ruthless old slave driver.'

'I'm glad you realize it,' Auntie called after our retreating backs.

We changed out of our school uniforms. I was ready before Jazz, and Geena was still in her room, so I climbed the ladder into the loft on my own. I wondered what Auntie had been doing, poking around up there. Was she looking for Mum's things? If she was, she wouldn't have found them. Her clothes and jewellery and everything else had been packed away and left at the back of her wardrobe and under the double bed. Taking them up to the loft had seemed like a very horrible, final act, a way of ending her life for ever. Admitting she was never coming back because all her things were out of sight and out of mind. I wondered if Auntie had persuaded Dad that it was time he moved them. It was just the kind of interfering thing she did best. She just couldn't seem to understand that it was better not to talk about things if it hurt too much. I was sure of that. Almost one hundred per cent sure.

When I climbed through the square hatch and breathed in the familiar musty smell, memories jumped out at me from all sides, spilling from the open boxes. Mum's stuff wasn't there, and I was glad. But there was my old fluffy toy cat, Billy, and my tatty old teddy with one eye. Geena's Boyzone T-shirt from years ago lay on the floor. There was Jazz's yellow baby blanket. She had to have it to tickle her nose with, or she couldn't get to sleep. Once Mum left it at a motorway service station when we were on the way home from Birmingham, and Dad had turned straight round and driven an extra thirty miles to get it back, while Jazz roared in the back seat.

My throat was suddenly hurting, and it wasn't because of the dust.

Dad hadn't heard me come up. He was standing at the back of the loft, stooping because of the angled roof, leafing through a photo album. I coughed gently.

'Amber!' Dad slammed the album shut like he'd been caught looking at dirty pictures. But I knew what it was. Our collection of Christmas photos, starting when Geena was a chubby, bouncing baby with a shock of dark hair sitting under a Christmas tree. The last picture was of me, Jazz and Mum in party hats, and Dad in a false nose and glasses he'd got out of a cracker. There hadn't been any photos last year.

'Auntie sent us up to help you,' I said. I searched his face. He looked tired and strained, and I felt unhappy, angry. This was all Auntie's fault. Couldn't she just leave us alone?

Dad nodded and stared down at the album in his hand. I prayed he wouldn't show it to me or even mention it. Then we heard Geena and Jazz at the bottom of the ladder, fighting over who'd got there first. Dad turned away and pushed the album under a pile of old clothes. I relaxed, suddenly conscious that I'd been holding my breath, and turned away as Geena and then Jazz climbed through the hatch. I didn't want to see if they had the sudden, explosive rush of memories that I'd had myself.

'Look at all this old junk,' Geena said in a too-casual voice.

'My Little Ponies.' Jazz pounced on a nearby box, and started pulling out plastic ponies with brightly coloured manes. 'I used to love these.'

Another memory flashed into my head. Jazz sitting on the living-room carpet, lining up her herd of ponies. Geena and I watching *EastEnders*. Mum ironing in the corner. It wasn't even an exciting memory, it wasn't anything special. So why did I feel like an invisible hand was twisting my insides this way and that?

Geena was poking around in a big box which stood an on old dressing table. 'Oh my God,' she said, pulling at a pink plastic arm. 'It's Dimple.' She lifted a large doll with long black hair out of the box. 'I thought she'd been thrown away ages ago.'

Dimple was named after a Bollywood film star, and she'd been Geena's favourite doll for years. Even when Geena pretended she didn't like dolls any more, Dimple had remained sitting on the end of her bed until she'd finally felt embarrassed about it. Geena had complained that there were no Indian dolls in the shops, so Mum had stuck one of her bindis in the middle of Dimple's plastic forehead. It was still there now, teardrop shaped, pink, edged with gold.

'I remember buying that doll,' Dad said, almost to himself.

We all knew the story because it was one of the family jokes. Geena, six years old and with a will of iron, had seen the doll in an expensive toy shop and had pestered Mum for ages to get it. Mum had refused. Eventually, a fed-up Dad had taken Geena out to buy her something to take her mind off the doll – 'something nice and cheap', he'd told Mum. They'd returned, Dad sheepish, Geena triumphant and carrying the doll.

'I'll never forget seeing Geena climbing out of the car with that doll in her arms,' Mum used to say. 'The box was nearly as big as she was.'

For a moment, Mum seemed very close. Closer than she'd been for months. A sort of breathless spell hung over us in the dusty loft. But none of us could bring ourselves to say her name.

'I thought your mum was going to kill me when we got home,' Dad blurted out. 'But she just laughed. She said she'd known all along that Geena would get her own way.'

We stood looking at each other. We all seemed suspended in our own personal bubbles of misery. Did we really want to break out of them? I wanted to talk about Mum. I wanted to so much that it shocked me. But then I saw tears in Dad's eyes. There's something terrible about seeing your parents crying; it shakes every bone in your body. So I did something else mature and grown-up instead. I panicked.

'Dinner must be ready,' I blurted out. 'I think I heard Auntie calling.'

'Yes, so did I,' Geena leaped in. She had Dimple clutched against her, and her face was in shadow. Jazz had already turned away and was climbing down the ladder as fast as she could.

We went downstairs in silence. Sneaking glances at the others, I could see that they all looked upset, especially Dad. Had I done the right thing or not? I was on such shaky ground, I didn't know. It seemed like everything was changing so fast, I couldn't keep up with it. We all knew whose fault that was. It didn't help make it better.

There was another shock waiting for me in the kitchen. Auntie was peeling potatoes at the sink and there at the table, looking cosily at home with a glass of orange juice in front of her, was Kim.

'What are you doing here?' I demanded.

'I just came round to say hi,' she mumbled.

'So why didn't you come and find me?' I asked pointedly.

Kim blushed. 'I was talking to Auntie – I mean, your aunt.'

Talking. Again. I glanced suspiciously at Auntie, but she had her back to me. What did they find to talk *about*?

'If dinner's not ready yet, I'm going to my study,' Dad said. 'I've got work to do.'

He sounded weary and defeated. Auntie noticed too. I saw her glance at him, but Dad deliberately didn't look at her. My heart leaped with hope. Auntie was definitely starting to get on Dad's nerves as well as ours. Maybe this was the beginning of the end . . .

'Let's go upstairs, Kim,' I said. It wasn't an invitation. It was an order.

Geena and Jazz wandered off into the living room to watch TV while Kim followed me dutifully upstairs. As soon as we were in my room, I shut the door and leaned my back against it.

'Now,' I said, 'give it up. What are you *really* doing here?'

Kim looked panicky. 'I told you, I came to see you. Everyone's talking about you and George Botley, and I just wanted to see if you were all right.'

'Thanks,' I said. 'Now the real reason.'

'Your auntie asked me to,' Kim muttered. She looked incredibly embarrassed, as well she might.

'Why?'

'I just happened to tell her – something,' said Kim, staring down at her feet.

'Is this anything to do with me?' I demanded.

'No.' Kim's blush deepened. 'It's about Gary.'

'Gary?' I frowned. 'Your mum's boyfriend? What's going on with him then?'

As soon as the words were out of my mouth, I felt my stomach twist and start to churn. Felt ice-cold all over. No. No, it *couldn't* be that.

'Kim.' I could hardly get the words out. 'It isn't – he isn't—'

Kim looked sick. 'No, not that!' she gasped. 'It's just – he keeps picking on me.'

Relief bloomed inside me like a flower. So it was just Kim getting paranoid as usual. For a minute, I'd been truly scared that something awful was going on.

'Oh, well,' I said, 'you've never liked him that much, have you? Maybe you should just keep out of his way.'

'I try,' Kim sighed. 'But he keeps calling me names. He says I'm useless.'

'Well, I call you that, sometimes,' I said, trying to jolly her along a bit.

Kim's sad eyes looked into mine. 'But you're my *friend*,' she said. 'I know you don't mean it.'

I felt like a worm.

'He keeps on and on and he won't shut up,' Kim said. Now that she'd started, it was as if a dam of emotion had burst open and she couldn't stop. 'And if I try to get away, he comes after me. And he pushed me. That's how I slipped and hurt my head. And my hand. He won't leave me alone. He keeps teasing and teasing . . .' Her sentence ended on a tearful gulp.

'And you told Auntie all this?'

Kim nodded. 'She said I should talk to Mum. I will, too.'

I stood there silently. Kim couldn't know how bad I was feeling. How long had this been going on for? I hadn't been interested in her problems. I didn't even know she had any problems. I thought it was just *Kim*.

It was a day for memories, and others slipped into my consciousness. Kim at Mum's funeral. The bunch of white daisies in her hand. She'd been a better friend than I deserved. And I was going to be nicer to her from now on.

'I think you should stop trying to get rid of your auntie.' Kim's voice, stronger now, broke into my thoughts.

I was as startled as if a fluffy little kitten had suddenly jumped up and scratched me, drawing blood. '*What?*'

'You should stop trying to marry Auntie off,' Kim said. 'She's nice. I like her.'

'You don't have to live with her,' I snapped.

'Give her a chance,' said Kim. 'She's only trying to help you.' She looked terrified and I knew she was going to say something earth-shattering. 'I bet your mum would be pleased she's here.'

I felt the colour bleach from my face. 'Kim—'

'She *would* be.' Now that Kim had decided to annoy me, she was really going for it. 'She'd be *glad* that someone was looking after you.'

Remembering what had happened in the loft, Dad's face, I felt a fiery surge of resentment which spilled over into my next words. 'Why don't you mind your own business?' But I put it a bit more rudely than that.

'All right then,' Kim said. 'I will.'

She got up and went over to the door. Her face was pale but her back was straight. I moved aside, and she went out without a backward glance. A minute later, I heard the front door slam.

*

'Kyra Hollins, your skirt is too short!' Mr Grimwade hollered. He was standing by the playground gate on Friday morning, pouncing on people as they went in. 'And Richard Martin, I do not want to see that nose stud, eyebrow ring and ten assorted earrings adorning your ugly face on Monday. Is that clear?'

'Lucky the teachers are pretty laid back about the inspectors arriving on Monday,' Geena remarked, walking into the playground. 'If they start to panic, we're in real trouble.' She said it just loudly enough for Mr Grimwade to hear. He gave the three of us a sidelong look, but said nothing.

'He's staring at us as if we're an unexploded bomb,' Jazz said.

'So is everyone else,' I added.

Everyone was looking as we strolled across the playground. They looked admiring, interested, puzzled or worried, depending on what kind of people they were. If anything, we were getting more attention than we'd ever got before. Geena claimed she'd had three boys ask her out face to face yesterday, and another four through go-betweens.

I saw Kim come through the gates, and fixed a smile to my face. I hadn't forgiven her for what she'd said, but I was prepared to meet her halfway and forgive her, eventually.

Kim stared through me with remarkable coolness. She skirted round the edge of the canteen and disappeared out of sight. My jaw dropped rather obviously.

'What's going on with you and Kim?' Geena demanded immediately. 'Have you two had a fight?'

'Don't be an idiot,' I snapped. Kim's behaviour had annoyed me more than I'd ever thought possible.

'Ooh, they *have*.' Jazz hopped from one foot to the other. 'Tell.'

I sighed, wondering how much I should reveal. 'She thought we should lay off Auntie,' I said. 'I told her no way.'

'There must have been something else,' Geena said shrewdly.

'Well . . .' I stared down at the ground. I wanted to tell them because I wanted them to be as mad as I was. 'She said that Mum would be glad that Auntie was around to look after us.'

Silence. All around us the noise of the playground boomed in our ears, but we said nothing.

'Got to go,' Geena said at last. 'See you.' She disappeared in a hurry. Jazz just turned and went off without a word.

For some reason I felt furious and upset. I kicked a nearby litter bin quite savagely, earning myself more sidelong looks. Chelsea and Sharelle were watching from the other side of the playground, their heads together. They didn't come over. I knew that they were talking about me.

Looking round to make sure as many people as

possible were watching, I pulled open a nearby door and walked into school. We were strictly not allowed in the building before the bell rang, and Grimwade usually posted teacher sentinels in the corridor to make sure. But this morning there was no one around. I headed for our classroom. I felt like doing something *really* annoying this morning. I didn't know what yet, but now would be a good time while no one was around.

Halfway down the corridor I stopped. I could hear voices. Cautiously I crept forward, my ears cocked. Our classroom door was ajar. I could hear Grimwade talking.

'. . . and what worries me most is if they're going to keep this behaviour up when the inspectors arrive on Monday.'

'I think they'll stop.' That was Mrs Kirke, Geena's form teacher. 'They're sensible girls.'

'I agree,' said Mr Arora. 'But maybe we should have another word with them.'

'Yes, it's a very delicate situation.' I recognized Mr Lucas, Jazz's form teacher. They were talking about *us*. Intrigued, I moved a little closer.

'Of course,' said Grimwade, 'we know *why* they're doing it.'

I almost gasped and had to clap my hand over my mouth. How could they possibly know about our marriage plans for Auntie and Mr Arora? They *couldn't*.

'It's been a traumatic year for them,' agreed Mrs Kirke. 'The stress was bound to come out sooner or later. They've been through so much and on the surface they seemed to be coping so well. It seems they've been fooling us all this time.'

'Maybe we could offer them some kind of grief counselling through the Schools' Psychology Service,' Mr Arora suggested.

For a moment I thought I was hearing things. Then I got it. They thought we'd gone off the rails because of *Mum*.

'It's not that, you idiots!' I wanted to yell. But I didn't. I crept away, back up the corridor. I was hot all over with this mad, intense rage. I was so *bored* with everyone else thinking they knew what was best for us. There was only one thing wrong with our lives. Auntie. Once she was gone, everything would be fine.

So they thought we were going to stop and go back to being perfect once the inspectors came. Had I got news for them. We were going to get worse. And I had the *best* idea where to start. The oh-so-special assembly on Monday morning.

CHAPTER 9

'I can't *believe* we did all that stuff,' Jazz said under her breath. 'Look, I'm so nervous, my hand's shaking.'

She attempted to put a silver bindi on her forehead and ended up with it stuck to her eyelashes.

'Don't be a drama queen,' I said, picking up my comb. 'It had to be done.'

'You don't think—' Geena began hesitantly. She was sprawled on Jazz's bed, watching us dress. 'You don't think we went a bit too far?'

My mind flew back two days to Friday afternoon. Sneaking into the hall after Ms Woods had set things up, we had prepared for an assembly that I guessed the inspectors would never forget. Today was Inderjit's wedding. Tomorrow could be our funeral.

'We *agreed*,' I said. 'We can't back out now.'

'I'm not backing out,' Geena snapped. Looking enormously irritated, she grabbed Jazz's pillow and heaved it at me. It hit me on the back of the head, almost shunting me through the dressing-table mirror.

147

'Stop it,' I shouted, throwing the comb at her.

'You two! You're like a couple of naughty kids,' Jazz moaned.

'You started it,' Geena and I snarled together. We were all on edge, unsurprisingly. And secretly, my row with Kim was still doing my head in. We hadn't made up yet and I couldn't believe how much it was bugging me.

I glared at Geena and Jazz and flounced out of the room, almost tripping over my long skirt. Out on the landing, though, I froze into stillness. I could hear Dad and Auntie talking in the living room. Not talking. Arguing.

'I know you think I'm interfering, Johnny—'

'Aren't you?' Dad sounded weary and defeated. I felt a pang of sympathy for him. 'Can't you just leave it alone? Things will work themselves out.'

'Will they?' Auntie asked. 'It's been a year, Johnny. It's too long already. I'm worried about the girls. And you. You never talk to them. You're never *here*, except when I nag you to come home from work early—'

'The office is very busy at the moment,' Dad retorted, a trace of anger in his voice.

'It's been busy for the last year, as far as I can tell,' Auntie broke in. 'When are things going to change? Because they can't go on like this. Buying the girls everything they want and never being here is not the solution—'

I jumped as Geena and Jazz came out of the bedroom behind me.

'What are you doing lurking around out here?' Geena demanded.

I shook my head at her but it was too late. Dad had heard us overhead, and was already halfway out of the front door.

'Girls, are you ready?' Auntie called.

We clattered downstairs. Auntie was wearing a peacock-blue sari stitched with gold swirls, and high-heeled sandals. Her hair was swept up on top of her head and pinned with two jewelled combs.

'You all look lovely,' she said approvingly.

'So do you,' Jazz blurted out. Geena and I were stunned, but Jazz seemed even more shocked than we were. She was so mortified, I didn't have the heart to kick her.

Dad was getting the car out of the garage, so we went to join him. He and Auntie were talking, but only just. They certainly weren't getting on very well at the moment. Dad had always been laid back, but you could only push him so far before he'd snap. It was all very hopeful.

We drove to Slough and then crawled up and down the road outside Inderjit's parents' house, looking for a parking space. The cars were double-, and in some cases treble-parked, and someone had even parked sideways with the bonnet of the car on the pavement.

'Who's the groom?' Geena asked, as Dad squeezed

the car between a Mercedes and a BMW, muttering a prayer under his breath.

'Harjinder's a doctor from Coventry,' Auntie replied. 'He has a younger brother, if you're interested.'

Geena looked outraged. I almost laughed but just managed to stop myself in time, and Jazz did actually give a kind of strangled snort.

The front of the house was decorated with flashing fairy lights. The door stood open, and people were spilling out to stand on the driveway. Bhangra music thumped and echoed down the street, played on an enormous sound system. As we approached the front door, we were patted on the head, pinched on the cheek and kissed and hugged by lots of people, some of whom I didn't actually know. I suppose most of them were some sort of relatives, but it's kind of hard to keep track when you have so many.

The house was controlled chaos. There were about twenty men in smart suits, some wearing turbans, crammed into the front room drinking whisky and all talking at once. Dad peeled off straight away to join them. We fought our way into the back room, where some aunties were watching a video of *Lagaan*. Auntie Rita and Biji were arguing in a corner, and Baby was in the garden, chatting up a teenage boy. The kitchen was heaving with women heating up samosas, handing out trays of tea and occasionally slapping one of the kids for misbehaving. There seemed to be hundreds of kids all over the place, playing, fighting, screaming, crying and generally getting on everyone's nerves. It was just like every other wedding I'd ever been to. Everybody was enjoying themselves enormously.

'Let's go see Inderjit,' Geena suggested.

The three of us stepped around a squawking toddler and headed upstairs. Auntie had already been absorbed into the group of women in the kitchen and was chattering away in Punjabi.

There were more kids fighting on the stairs, but eventually we made it to the top. There was another bunch of them in Inderjit's parents' bedroom. Two girls were pulling sari after sari out of a wardrobe like magicians, while a little boy was parading around with a big pair of white underpants on his head. Inderjit's door was closed, so Geena tapped on it loudly. Sukhvinder, Inderjit's sister, opened it.

'Oh, it's you,' she said with a grin. 'Indira, it's Geena, Amber and Jazz.'

'Yeah, they're all right,' Inderjit called. 'Let them in.'

The bedroom was full of girls dressed up like colourful, painted butterflies in floaty, pastel-coloured saris and shalwar kameez. Inderjit was sitting on the bed in her sari underskirt and tight top. Her hands and feet had already been intricately patterned with mehndi, and one of her cousins was weaving white flowers into her long dark hair. Lucky it had grown back, really.

'Hi,' I said. 'Did you know there's a fire under your bed?'

Inderjit gave a shriek, bobbed down and retrieved a lit cigarette. 'I thought you might be my mum,' she said.

'Your husband won't like you smoking,' one of the girls teased.

'He knows what he can do,' Inderjit retorted. The girls giggled and started making rude comments about the groom and the wedding night in Punjabi.

'Inderjit, *beti*,' called a voice from outside the door.

'God, that *is* my mum!' Looking panicky, Inderjit threw the cigarette out of the open window onto the driveway. We heard a faint *'Ow!'* below us.

'You scored a direct hit on Uncle Davinder,' remarked Jazz, who was nearest to the window.

Inderjit's mum had come to hurry things along because we were late for the gurdwara. We were shooed out of the room so that Inderjit could be wound into her sari, and then we hung around outside the house so that we could see her emerge in all her glory. She came out looking doe-eyed and innocent, as if she'd never shaved her head or smoked a ciggie in her life.

'Let's make a dash for it,' Dad said in a low voice. 'It's going to be hell trying to get a parking space at the gurdwara.'

Everyone else had the same idea, and there was a mad rush to the cars. Dad just doesn't have that killer instinct when it comes to parking, so we had to leave the car three streets away. We hurried to the gurd-wara, which was an old church hall, and joined the end of the queue at the doors. Once inside, we took off our shoes and left them on the racks.

People were moving along the aisle down the middle of the hall to bow to the Holy Book, which was under a gold canopy at the far end. When we'd done that, we split up, Dad to sit on the men's side and us on the women's. I sat down cross-legged on the floor and looked around. The bride and groom were already sitting at the front with the priest, but people were still coming in from outside.

I looked at my watch. Twenty-two hours to go to the special assembly and then we'd be dead. I was still sure we'd done the right thing. Fairly sure. About fifty per cent, really. Or maybe thirty.

More people were coming in down the aisle. I watched idly as Mr Arora walked past me.

Mr Arora?

What was *he* doing here?

My eyes almost fell out of my head. It was like seeing a dream suddenly become real. Mr Arora was *here*. I didn't know why or how. I didn't care. This was our chance, and we were going to grab it.

I glanced at Geena and Jazz sitting either side of me. Geena was examining her nails and Jazz was fiddling with her hair. I elbowed them both in the ribs simultaneously.

'Mr Arora's here,' I whispered.

'What?' Jazz hadn't heard what I said.

'Nice try, Amber.' Geena yawned, not looking up.

'He *is*.' I looked round, but he seemed to have disappeared. 'Where's he gone?'

For a moment I was worried. Maybe my brain was overheating and I was hallucinating. Then I spotted him sitting down not far from Dad. 'There he is,' I whispered. 'Near Dad, next to the guy in the hideous purple and green tie.'

'That's Mr Arora!' Jazz gasped.

'That's what I've been trying to tell you,' I said.

We all stared at Mr Arora's handsome profile, willing him to turn round and see us. He didn't.

'Do you think he's going to the reception?' Geena asked.

We looked sideways at Auntie. The same thought was in all our minds.

'Let's hope so,' I said.

'Maybe we shouldn't wait to find out,' Jazz said anxiously. 'Maybe we should just grab him afterwards and push him in Auntie's direction.'

From then on, I paid no attention to the wedding at all. I fixed my eyes on Mr Arora, watching his every move. Not that he did much. He looked at his watch four times, ran his hand through his hair twice and scratched his arm once. By the end of the ceremony I was a nervous wreck.

'Listen,' I whispered, as everyone rose to their feet.

'You two keep Auntie here while I grab Mr Arora and bring him over to meet her.'

I scrambled to get up, almost tripping over my floaty scarf. But as I attempted to launch myself across the aisle towards Mr Arora, one of Inderjit's aunties, well over a hundred kilos and dressed in a lime-green sari, sailed into my path like a battleship, all guns blazing.

'There you are,' she boomed, pinching my cheek and nearly taking the top layer of skin off. 'I thought you weren't here. Come and give your auntie a hug.'

I was crushed against her enormous stomach, and released, dazed and bruised, about ten seconds later. Jazz was trying to hide behind Auntie, but neither she nor Geena escaped. By the time we'd all come up for air there were so many people milling around us, we couldn't see Mr Arora at all.

'Let's get straight to the reception.' Dad had appeared next to us, looking harassed. 'We might have a chance of a parking space if we run.'

'What about Mr Arora?' Geena mouthed at me as we raced out of the gurdwara.

'He'll be at the reception,' I said confidently, hoping I was right.

The reception was held in a hall about a mile away. By cutting through the backstreets and jumping one red light (Geena said it was two, but Dad swore the second one was amber), we reached the hall and nicked the last space in the car park. I glanced round as we went in, but I couldn't see Mr Arora's car.

The hall was filling up fast. It had been decorated with streamers and garlands of flowers, which some of the kids were already dismantling and chucking at each other. There were tables everywhere, and the harassed caterers were rushing out of the kitchen and plonking silver dishes of crisps, peanuts, samosas, pakoras and bhajis on them, which were pounced on and scoffed in five seconds flat. Dad headed straight for the bar in the corner. There was a dance floor in the middle of the hall, and a band was setting up on stage.

'Stop checking out the lead singer and look for Mr Arora,' I instructed Geena. 'Where's Jazz got to?'

Jazz had got left behind somewhere in the crowd surging forward for food. She bobbed up at my elbow about a minute later, grinning widely. 'Mr Arora's over there by the door,' she said in a stage whisper. 'What are you going to do?'

'Ask him if he wants to marry Auntie,' I said. 'Don't be *stupid*. I'll get him to come over and meet her. You hang onto her. Don't let her go anywhere.'

I pushed my way through the crowd as the band began to play. Rocky, one of Inderjit's cousins who's quite good looking but thinks he's so *it*, tried to grab my hand and pull me onto the dance floor, but I avoided him with a sweet smile.

Mr Arora was standing near the door talking to a

couple of men I didn't know. I went over and touched his arm.

'Amber.' He stared down at me, his face crinkling into a warm smile. 'Hello, what are you doing here?'

'Inderjit's my cousin, sir,' I said. 'I didn't expect to see *you* either.'

He laughed. 'I was at college with Harry, the groom.'

'Oh.' That explained that. 'Would you like to come and meet my aunt, sir?'

All right, it was a bit upfront, but he was hardly going to say no, was he?

'That would be lovely,' Mr Arora replied politely.

Dizzy with triumph, I led him across the dance floor. Heads turned as we made our way to the other side of the hall. He was *so* good looking, it was impossible not to imagine Auntie falling at his feet. And she looked all right too. It was going to work, I was sure.

Geena and Jazz had cornered Auntie, managing to get her away from the gaggle of gossipy women she was talking to. They were looking around for a free table when I stepped forward, smiling innocently.

'Auntie, this is my teacher, Mr Arora,' I said smoothly. 'He's a friend of Inderjit's husband.'

'Pleased to meet you,' Mr Arora said with that winning smile. Auntie smiled back. They stared into each other's eyes. I almost expected to hear a Bollywood love song playing in the background, but the band were actually belting out very loud bhangra with a techno beat.

'I think I see a free table,' Geena said. 'We'll go and save it, Auntie.'

I nodded. Leave them alone together. Great idea. Geena and I turned and went off, but had to go back and remove Jazz, who was still there, grinning knowingly from one to the other.

'Ow!' Jazz complained as we carried her away by her elbows. 'I wanted to hear what they were saying.'

'They're not going to get all lovey-dovey if you're standing there with your ears flapping,' I said.

We sat down at the table and kept watch. At first, everything went well. Mr Arora and Auntie were talking, their heads together. They seemed oblivious to all the noise around them. They were smiling. It was looking good.

'Shall we get up and dance?' said Geena, who had one eye on Auntie and Mr Arora, and the other on the singer who, admittedly, was very fit and looked like an Indian Leonardo DiCaprio.

'No, wait,' I said.

Something had happened. It had all changed. Auntie took a step backwards, frowning. She was waving her hands around a bit. Mr Arora looked puzzled. Then he frowned too. Auntie put her hands on her hips and began talking at speed. Mr Arora folded his arms and tapped his foot.

'That's not good body language,' remarked Jazz, staring intently.

'God, they're *arguing*,' Geena said.

'No, they *can't* be,' I groaned.

They were arguing. Why, I don't know. Words were being tossed back and forth between them now and things were getting heated. We saw Auntie snap out a final retort and, with a swirl of her peacock-blue sari, turn away and head in our direction. Her face was grim. Mr Arora, looking like he did after he'd just had a run-in with George Botley, stalked off in the opposite direction.

'I don't think they like each other,' Jazz said, aghast.

'But they *have* to.' I felt sick. Our plans were tumbling down in ruins.

'Who's that guy your aunt was talking to?' Dad appeared at the table, clutching a tray of soft drinks. 'I don't think I know him.'

'My teacher,' I said shortly.

Dad's eyebrows shot up. 'Your *teacher*?' he repeated. 'But it looked as if they were *arguing*.'

'They were.' I seized the opportunity to stick the knife in and twist it. 'I just wish Auntie would stop interfering, Dad. I don't know what she's been saying to Mr Arora, but she could make things really tough for me at school.'

Dad's lips tightened as Auntie reached our table. 'What were you saying to Amber's teacher?' he asked without preamble.

'Nothing.' Auntie looked more furious than I'd ever seen her before. 'I've met those kind of guys

159

before. They think they know it all, but they don't know anything.'

She took a glass from the tray and walked off, leaving us all stunned. Looking worried and angry, Dad went after her.

'So that's that then,' Jazz said flatly. 'We're stuck with her.'

'Oh no.' Geena slumped down on the table with her head in her hands.

'All right,' I said, rallying a bit even though I was shocked. 'It's bad, but not that bad. Arora's out. But we can look around for someone else.'

'It's not that.' Geena raised a tragic face. 'Don't you realize what we've *done*?'

Jazz and I looked at her blankly.

'All that stuff we've done for tomorrow,' Geena went on. 'The *assembly*. It was all for nothing. Now we're going to get into the biggest trouble of our whole lives. For *nothing*.'

CHAPTER 10

'Jazz, don't forget the music stands,' I panted. I was heaving the right backdrops into place after we'd spent ages adding scenes from *Aladdin* on Friday. We'd come to school very early so we had time to put things right. We'd had to persuade the caretaker to let us in, though, by claiming that there were some last-minute adjustments to be made for the assembly. He didn't buy that, so we'd threatened to set Ms Woods on him, which is enough to put the fear of God into anyone. 'Did you remember to bring the screwdriver?'

Jazz nodded, taking it from her pocket. She went over to the music stands stacked in the corner of the hall, and began to tighten up the screws that held the stands together.

'I hope we don't forget anything,' she said nervously.

'I've got a list.' Geena whipped a piece of paper from her bag and waved it at us. She was removing some of the acetate sheets from the overhead projector – we'd added a few alternative, ruder lyrics to the songs we were going to sing.

'That was efficient,' I said, heading towards the

piano. There was a whoopee cushion under Mrs Murray's seat and we'd stuck the piano lid tightly shut with loads of Blu-tak.

'I couldn't sleep for worrying last night,' Geena explained. 'So I got up and wrote the list.'

'Don't forget the punk metal CD we put in the sound system,' I reminded her. 'I hid the proper one behind the stereo.'

Geena bobbed behind the curtain and came out again a moment later with the CD in her hand.

'I wonder if Dad and Auntie will have made up by the time we get home tonight,' she remarked, stepping down from the stage.

Dad and Auntie hadn't spoken to each other since the wedding reception incident with Mr Arora the previous afternoon. I'd stirred it a bit, too, by moaning to Dad about how difficult my life at school would be as a result.

'I hope not,' I replied. If Auntie and Dad were fighting, it might be our only way of getting rid of her now.

'I'm glad we didn't saw through the head's chair legs like I suggested,' Jazz said. 'We'd never have been able to repair those.'

'I can't lift this,' I gasped, struggling with the piano lid. 'Give me a hand.'

All three of us pushed and heaved at the piano. Eventually the lid popped open, and we began scraping off the Blu-tak.

'I can't believe we did this,' Jazz said soberly. 'Are we mad?'

'We had a good reason,' I reminded her.

'I know.' Jazz glanced sideways at me. 'But . . .' She cleared her throat awkwardly. I knew that something quite shocking was coming and I had a fair idea what it was going to be. 'Apart from Auntie, didn't you kind of *enjoy* it?'

'I don't know what you mean,' Geena said unconvincingly.

'Oh yes, you do,' Jazz retorted. 'I don't know about you, but I'm fed up with trying to be perfect all the time. I just want to be *me*.'

'Oh God,' I said. 'What a prospect.'

Jazz stuck her tongue out. 'I don't mean that I want to behave like this all the time. I'm just tired of trying to pretend to everyone that everything's OK when it isn't.' She came to a full stop and stared wide-eyed at Geena and me.

'All right,' Geena admitted. 'I *do* know what you mean.'

'And I think we should stop trying to get Auntie married off, too,' Jazz mumbled, staring down at her feet. 'It's got us into loads of trouble so far, and all this' – she waved her hand around the hall – 'would have got us *suspended*.'

'You know, I think she's right,' agreed Geena soberly. 'Much as I hate to admit it. We'd better just drop it, Amber. It was a stupid idea.'

'It was *my* idea,' I reminded her.

Geena raised her eyebrows at me. 'I rest my case.'

'The teachers think we started all this stuff because of Mum,' I blurted out, surprising even myself. 'They think we might need help or counselling or something.'

For once Jazz and Geena did not look away or run off. They both regarded me thoughtfully.

'What do *you* think?' Geena asked, looking at me intently.

The hall doors flew open, and we all nearly jumped out of our skins. Ms Woods stood there. Her hair was as wild as ever and she looked on the verge of hysteria.

'Oh, hello, girls,' she said, eyeing us a bit warily. 'I just popped in to make sure everything's ready. But I see you beat me to it.'

'Yes, miss,' Geena said, sliding the CD smoothly into her pocket. 'Everything's fine.'

We helped Ms Woods set out some more chairs. There wasn't time for us to talk any more, and we hadn't really said anything earth-shattering. But somehow I felt better. Lighter. As if someone had come along and lifted a huge weight off my back.

Five inspectors turned up, but they were a bit disappointing. As Mr Morgan, the headteacher, marched into the school hall with the inspectors behind him, everyone sat up to get a better look. Geena, Jazz and I were on the stage behind the curtains with the rest of the assembly cast, and we were all fighting to get a peek. After all the build-up, we were expecting them to look like gangsters or film stars. But there was a mousy woman in a blue suit, and four men who looked like rejects from Mrs Dhaliwal's marriage file. They sat down, poker-faced, and waited to be entertained.

'They don't look like inspectors,' Jazz muttered, as Ms Woods flapped around giving us a last-minute pep talk.

Ms Woods rushed up to us, crackling with tension. 'Geena, are you ready to give the introduction?' she hissed. 'Amber, the backdrop. Everybody else, stand by!'

Looking perfectly calm and composed, Geena glided out onto the stage. Her voice was clear and confident as she stood in front of a large map, showing the spread of world religions, and read out the short introduction about how the assembly was to celebrate the diversity of religions and cultures in our school. Meanwhile, I took up my position at the ropes that controlled the backdrops.

'Christians!' whispered Ms Woods, sounding about as friendly as a Roman gladiator in the Coliseum. 'On stage now!'

Paul Bruford, Katie Heaps and Jackson Jones shuffled out onto the stage, looking terrified. Quickly I began to haul at the ropes to change the backdrop to one of St Paul's Cathedral. Unfortunately, nothing happened. I pulled again, frantically this time. Still no change.

'Amber!' Ms Woods called urgently from the other side of the stage. I'm sure everyone in the hall heard her. I wouldn't have been surprised if they'd heard her at the end of the street. There was a loud gasp from the audience, which chilled me. After our recent display of behaving badly, they thought I was doing this *on purpose*.

I began to sweat as I realized that somehow I'd messed up, while rushing to change the backdrops earlier that morning. All I could do, as I worked to untangle the ropes, was close my eyes and pray that Widow Twankey's kitchen didn't appear when I pulled.

I pulled. St Paul's Cathedral unfurled before my eyes, and my knees wobbled with relief. The teachers looked relieved too, although some of the pupils seemed quite disappointed.

'You do enjoy living on the edge, don't you, Amber?' Geena remarked, as we lined up to replace the Christians, who were trooping off-stage looking relieved.

'Danger's my middle name,' I said airily, trying to still my madly beating heart.

'We're on,' Jazz whispered.

After that tiny hiccup, everything went smoothly. The inspectors remained poker-faced throughout the whole assembly, but they must have been quite impressed. Even Daniel Cohen remembered his words.

As we all filed out of the hall afterwards, there was a definite atmosphere of cautious confidence throughout the school. Even Mr Grimwade was looking pleased and baring his teeth at everyone. It felt like we'd met the challenge head-on and we were going to survive it. And as we went back to class, Kim smiled at me for the first time in ages. That made me feel better too.

However, there was something unpleasant but necessary that had to be done. At break time, when everyone had gone outside, I went to speak to Mr Arora. He was sitting in his classroom marking books, and he looked up at me wearily as I approached. There were black circles under his eyes, and I wondered if he'd got any sleep last night at all.

'Sir,' I said hesitantly, 'I just wanted to say – I'm sorry for everything that happened last week. It won't happen again.'

Mr Arora looked at me quizzically for a while. 'I'm very glad to hear it,' he said at last. 'And, Amber, it's not surprising. You've had a very tough time over the last year.'

'Yes.' I couldn't even get the 'sir' out because my throat was tight.

'And you must know that if you ever want to talk, I'm always available,' he added gently.

What I really wanted to know was why he'd had a row with Auntie at Inderjit's wedding. But I couldn't ask that.

'So . . .' Mr Arora began fiddling with a paperclip. 'Your auntie lives with you now?'

'Yes, sir.'

'I see.' I didn't know what he saw, and he wasn't going to tell me either. He pushed back his chair and stood up. 'We'll discuss this again when we've got a bit more time. Off you go now.'

I went out into the corridor. Why Auntie had rowed with Mr Arora didn't matter now anyway. We'd decided not to try and get her married off. That left us with a bit of a situation, though. Was Auntie now here to stay? It was something I would have to discuss with the others.

As I turned the corner, I bumped into Geena, who was coming out of her form room.

'What are you doing here?' she asked. 'The bell went ages ago.'

'I could ask you the same question,' I said.

Geena looked a tiny bit embarrassed. 'I've just been apologizing to Mrs Kirke,' she said. 'I thought it was the right thing to do.'

'So did I,' I assured her. 'I've just come from Mr Arora.'

'Oh, good,' Geena said, relieved. 'Do you think if we twist Jazz's arm enough, she'll say sorry to Mr Lucas?'

'Let's ask her.'

Jazz was standing in a corner of the playground on her own. Her eyes were suspiciously pink and she was sniffing.

'What's up?' Geena asked, handing her a tissue. 'You don't have to examine it. It *is* clean.'

'I've just been talking to Mr Lucas,' Jazz sniffled. 'He was really *nice* to me. We talked about Mum and everything.'

Geena and I put our arms round her. My lip was wobbling and Geena looked bright and teary round the eyes. In a moment we'd all be bawling, and this wasn't the time or the place.

We were saved by Kim, who was coming slowly towards us, her face pink, as if she wasn't sure of her welcome. Geena nodded at me, whispered, 'Make it up,' and led a gulping Jazz away.

'Are you all right?' Kim asked shyly.

I nodded. 'Don't worry. We've given up behaving badly. You were right. It was a stupid idea.'

'Oh.' Kim looked relieved.

'What about Gary?' I asked. 'Did you talk to your mum?'

Kim beamed as if a light had been switched on inside her. 'Yeah, I did. You'll never guess what, she'd decided to chuck him anyway. He's gone. For good.'

'That's great.' I gave her a big hug. I'd never done that before, but she looked pleased.

A snigger from behind interrupted us. George Botley stood there, his eyes popping out. 'What are you two up to?' he grinned.

I walked up to him and stood nose-to-nose. 'George,' I said, 'you're not going to get anywhere while you're the class joke. And no girl's going to look at you twice. So you'd better take a long, hard look at yourself, and start shaping up.'

I led Kim away across the playground. We left George open-mouthed and red-faced, gawping after us.

'*You're* not going to go out with him, are you?' Kim asked in awe.

'No way,' I said. 'But it's given him something to think about.'

By the time I met up with Geena and Jazz at the end of the day, we all looked and felt happier. But we didn't say anything about what had happened until we'd left Kim at the flats and walked on. Then there was something else to sort out.

'What are we going to do about Auntie?' I asked.

Geena gave me a stern look. 'I thought we'd decided not to try and find her a husband.'

'Fine,' I agreed. 'She might get married anyway, sometime, and move out. But what are we going to do *now*?'

Jazz looked alarmed. 'If you've got any more dumb ideas, Amber, just keep them to yourself.'

'As a matter of fact, I haven't,' I admitted. 'Not a single, solitary one.'

'So what are you saying?' Geena asked briskly.

I knew what we had to do. I just didn't want to admit it. 'I'm saying that I haven't got any more ideas.'

'Which means,' Geena persisted ruthlessly, 'that Auntie's here, she's staying and we have to get used to it.'

'Oh, let's not go that far,' I cut in. 'We'll give her a *chance*, that's all.'

'And what if she still gets on our nerves after six months?' Jazz asked doubtfully.

'Er – I'm sure I'll have another idea by then,' I mumbled.

Geena shook her head. 'Admit it, Amber,' she said. 'Auntie isn't going anywhere. There's only one thing for it and, believe me, I don't like it any more than you do.' She took a deep breath. 'We'll have to try and get along with her.'

'Are you kidding?' Jazz shrieked.

'Have you got any better ideas?' demanded Geena.

Jazz looked sullen. 'No. But I'd rather cut my ears off.'

'Then you won't get your second holes,' I pointed out.

Jazz couldn't help laughing. 'But will she try to get along with *us*?' she asked.

'If you mean, will she let us stay up late and live on

takeaways and get away with murder, then, no,' Geena replied. 'But then, Mum wouldn't have done that either, would she?'

Jazz and I were silent. Almost without knowing it, we'd kind of slipped into a routine over the past three weeks. Thinking back, it reminded me of when Mum was there. If I was perfectly honest, I knew that Geena was right and that Mum would have behaved almost exactly the same as Auntie about bed times and boring stuff like that. We'd only got away with so much over the last year because Dad had been so out of it.

'Does that mean we have to be nice to her though?' I asked, only half joking.

'We're teenagers,' Geena replied. 'That means we don't have to be nice to anyone.'

'Amber's not a teenager yet and neither am I,' Jazz remarked.

'You behave like one,' I told her.

'Do I?' Jazz looked pleased, then frowned.

Dad's car was outside the house again when we got home. But we were so used to it by now, nobody commented. He came out of the living room as we let ourselves in, and one look at his face made my stomach lurch sickeningly. He looked as if he'd been crying.

'Dad, what's the matter?' Geena asked.

He stared emptily at us. 'I had a row with your auntie,' he said. 'She's gone.'

CHAPTER 11

'Gone?' I repeated. 'What do you mean?'

'She packed up and left in a taxi a few minutes ago,' Dad said. 'I don't know where she's gone.'

A great wave of fury rushed over me. She'd *gone*? When the going got rough, she'd just upped and left? I had Auntie down as many things, but not a quitter.

'You mean, she's not coming back?' Jazz asked, arriving into the conversation late as usual.

Dad shook his head helplessly.

'Dad, what did you argue about?' Geena asked.

He shrugged. 'You girls. The way she was inter-fering. I knew you didn't like it. I knew you found it hard.'

None of us could speak.

'I found it hard too,' Dad went on. 'I didn't want to be reminded—' He cleared his throat and tried again, took his glasses off and put them back on. 'I didn't want to be reminded of what happened to your mum.'

'Maybe Auntie was right though,' I said, forcing the words out past the lump stuck in my throat.

'Perhaps we *should* have talked about it.'

'Maybe we'd feel better if we did,' Geena agreed. Jazz nodded.

We stood there looking helplessly at each other. It was difficult to know where to start.

'Right.' Dad squared his shoulders, looking more together than he'd been for a long time. 'The first thing I need to do is try to sort things out with your aunt. I'm going out to look for her.'

'We'll come too,' I began. But Dad shook his head.

'You three wait here,' he told us. 'She might phone. We'll talk when I get back.'

And I knew that, at last, he meant *talk*. Then he did something he hadn't done for ages. He hugged each one of us tightly for a long time. It felt as if we were climbing a tall mountain and we were very close to the summit. By leaving, Auntie had finally achieved what she wanted. We were *talking*.

The door shut behind Dad. Without a word to the others, I turned away and slipped upstairs. I didn't know why, but I knew where I was going.

I passed my bedroom and peeked in. The bed had been stripped, and the wardrobe doors stood open. The wardrobe was empty except for coat hangers.

I went into Mum and Dad's bedroom. I kneeled on the floor and pulled a familiar, blue suitcase out from under the bed. It was covered in dust which I smoothed away with my fingers before unlocking it.

The perfume that hit me made the tears start in my

eyes before I even saw Mum's clothes. Flowery and familiar, it wafted into the bedroom and lingered around me. I put my head down on the gold sari which lay on top of the case and began to cry.

I cried until my face was raw and aching and my eyes were swollen. It seemed like hours but in reality it was only a few minutes, I think. And when I wiped the tears from my face at last, I felt better. As if I had finally climbed to the top of that mountain.

I plunged my hands into the pool of saris. Scarlet, royal blue, deep purple, pinks, golds, creams, tangerines and citrus, they flowed around me in silks and satins and chiffons, until I was surrounded by colour. Underneath were piles of letters and other bits of paper.

I picked one of the letters up and idly glanced at it. Instantly I was transfixed. I read the next one and the next. It was a gorgeous and moving love story, like a Bollywood film but real. Letters from years ago, before we were born. Letters between Mum and Dad, Dad and Auntie, Mum and Auntie, Dad and his parents. And as I read them, I began to understand everything that had happened.

There were other, newer airmail letters. These were even more startling. I was deep in one of them when a noise at the door made me glance up. Geena was standing there looking at me.

'What—?' she began, but that was as far as she got. Her face was already crumpling as she stared at

175

Mum's saris. She stumbled into the room, sobbing quietly.

Jazz came up behind her to see what was going on. She didn't even have a chance to say anything before her mouth turned down and she began crying too. That started me off again. We all sat on the floor and sobbed.

After a few minutes there was silence. Not a strained silence, but a peaceful one.

'What are you doing?' Geena asked, pointing at the letters in my hand.

'I've been reading them,' I replied. 'Now I know why Auntie and Mum didn't like each other.'

'You've been reading other people's letters?' Geena asked sternly.

'Go on, tell us,' Jazz said.

'Well, if Geena doesn't want me to . . .'

Geena thumped my arm. 'Go on.'

I curled up into a ball, hugging my knees. 'Dad was going to marry Auntie's best friend. It was all arranged. Then he met Mum and he called it all off and married her instead.'

Geena and Jazz stared at me. '*Dad* did?' Geena said. 'I didn't think he had it in him.'

'Well, he did,' I replied. 'And that's why Mum and Auntie didn't like each other.' I handed them a couple of letters. 'This one's from Dad to Biji and Babaji. It tells them he's going to marry Mum. And how much he loves her.'

'Go, Dad!' Jazz said. She pulled a hideous face. 'I'm glad Auntie's gone then, the miserable old cow. Good riddance.'

'Hold on,' I said. 'There's more.' I picked up a handful of letters. 'Mum wrote to Auntie when she knew – what was going to happen to her. She *asked* her to come and look after us.'

Geena and Jazz's faces were a study. If I hadn't been so deadly serious, I would have found it funny.

'You've absolutely got to be kidding,' Geena said at last.

'No. These are the letters Auntie wrote back to her.' I handed them over. 'It's perfectly clear.'

Geena unfolded the letters with shaking hands and skimmed through them. 'Amber's right,' she said at last.

'Omigod.' Jazz looked stricken. 'And we were so *mean* to her.'

Geena groaned. 'Mum would kill us if she knew what we'd done.'

'Well, Auntie didn't exactly break a leg to get over here, did she?' Jazz pointed out defensively. 'I mean, it took her a *year* to come.'

'I suppose she *did* have a life in India she had to sort out first,' Geena replied. 'You know, her job and her house and all that.'

I was ashamed. I'd never given a single thought to what Auntie had had to sacrifice to come to Britain. Job, house, friends, a whole life of her own.

That's what made up my mind. 'Maybe there's still time to stop her,' I said, and jumped to my feet.

'What do you mean?' Geena looked perplexed. 'It must be half an hour since Dad said she'd left.'

I glanced at the clock on the wall. 'It is,' I replied. 'But you know what the traffic on the Broadway's like at this time of day. We might just catch her.'

'Dad told us to stay here—' Jazz began.

'We've got our mobiles,' I broke in. 'We can text him and tell him where we are.'

'But we don't know where Auntie's gone,' Geena grumbled. 'She could be going to the airport or to a hotel or to one of the relatives. She could be any-where.'

'Not if she's stuck in the traffic.' I ran over to the door with Jazz at my heels. 'Come on, it's worth a go, isn't it? Or do you want to feel guilty for the rest of your life?'

Geena looked guilty already. 'No, of course not.'

We dashed downstairs and outside. There we came to a halt on the doorstep.

'If the driver was heading to the Broadway, he'd go that way,' Jazz said, pointing down the street.

'But if he was taking a short cut,' I said, 'he'd have gone the opposite way.'

Geena threw her hands in the air. 'I *knew* this was a bad idea.'

'If you're looking for your aunt,' said a timid voice behind us, 'the taxi went off that way.'

178

We turned to find Mrs Macey blinking at us from behind her glasses. She was pointing with her trowel down the street in the direction of Mr Attwal's shop.

'Er – thanks,' I said.

'I saw your aunt when she left.' Mrs Macey's eyes behind the thick lenses were very shrewd, and I wondered how much she'd guessed. 'She said she was going back to India.'

We glanced anxiously at each other.

'Not if we can help it,' Geena said.

'Good luck,' Mrs Macey called after us as we dashed down the path. It hardly surprised us because it had been kind of a surprising day all round.

We ran towards the corner. Mr Attwal was sitting outside the shop, deep in his computer manual. He looked up when he heard our footsteps.

'If you're looking for your aunt, you just missed her,' he called as we raced past him. 'She left me about ten minutes ago.'

We skidded to a halt so fast, it's amazing sparks didn't shoot up from our trainers.

'She was here?' I panted.

Mr Attwal nodded. 'She saw me sitting outside so she stopped the cab, and we had a long chat. Shame she's leaving us, isn't it?'

I turned to Geena and Jazz. 'That means we've got a good chance of catching her,' I said, thanking heaven that Mr Attwal could talk all the legs off a donkey. 'Which way did they go?'

'That way.' Mr Attwal pointed in the direction of the Broadway.

We set off again. The traffic was already building up in the backstreets. It was stopping and starting but it was still moving. It was hard to tell how far Auntie might have got. We ran along the pavement, looking for taxis.

'There she is!' Geena yelled triumphantly, darting forward. A black taxi with KRISHNA CABS printed on the door was sitting in a queue of cars. Geena leaned forward through the open passenger window and an old granny in a white sari let out a stream of angry Punjabi. Geena jumped backwards as the taxi moved on.

'It wasn't her,' she mumbled.

As we ran along the pavement, a boy on a bike drew up alongside, keeping pace with us. It was Leo.

'Hey,' he said.

'Hi,' I responded, not stopping.

'All right?' Leo added.

'Sure,' I said.

'Where's your aunt going?'

I came to a dead stop and Geena and Jazz charged into the back of me. 'You've *seen* Auntie?' I asked as I picked myself up from the pavement.

Leo nodded. 'About five minutes ago in a taxi in Scotland Street. I waved, but she didn't see me.'

'Did you see which way the taxi went?' I asked.

'It turned right into Portman Road and then went

up King Street,' Leo replied promptly. 'It looked like the driver was taking a short cut to the Broadway.'

'Thanks.' I smiled and fluttered my eyelashes at him.

'See you later, yeah?' he called after us as we ran on.

'My, my,' said Geena. 'You *are* popular, Amber.'

'Can we please concentrate on finding Auntie?' I said snootily.

The traffic was queuing up Scotland Street and into Portman Road. Everything had stopped for a red light, although it probably wasn't moving much anyway. From the bottom of the street I could see that a black cab had pulled up next to the kerb. A girl was standing on the kerb, leaning in through the open window, talking to someone inside.

'That's Kim!' Jazz and I said together.

At that very moment Kim moved away from the cab, and it edged its way back into the line of traffic. Kim waved as it shot off round the corner onto the Broadway. Then she walked off in the opposite direction.

'Quick!' Geena urged. 'We have to catch them before the driver turns off the Broadway or we'll lose them.'

We dashed down the street. A carload of young Indian boys in a BMW started hitting the horn and whistling at us, and we lost a few seconds when Geena slowed down to check them out. By the time we got to the corner, the traffic had started moving up the Broadway towards the underpass at the end.

I groaned. 'If we don't catch it before the under-pass, we're done for.'

The Broadway was an obstacle course. Many of the shopkeepers had tables outside their shops selling everything from fruit and vegetables to saris. And it was full of people. We skipped from one side of the pavement to the other like boxers in training.

'Oof!' Jazz panted as she bumped into a large lady in a pink sari. 'Sorry.'

'They're nearly at the underpass,' I said, shading my eyes. We were close behind now, but would we make it in time? I didn't think so.

Then, suddenly, the cab swerved to the left. There was a barrage of angry hoots and shouts from the drivers behind it as the brakes screeched and it pulled up onto the kerb.

The door opened and Auntie got out. She stood on the pavement with people milling around her, watching us as we hurried towards her.

'You took your time,' she said with a faint smile. 'Lucky I spotted you in the driver's mirror.'

I bent over, trying to relieve the stitch in my side. 'You mean – you were *expecting* us to come after you?' I wheezed.

Auntie shrugged. 'I hoped you might. But I wasn't sure at all.'

'What if we hadn't?' I asked.

'I don't know,' Auntie replied.

We stood there awkwardly while people milled

around us. Even Auntie looked embarrassed. We weren't going to throw our arms around each other and forgive and forget. But we had to start somewhere.

'We know about Mum asking you to come and look after us,' Jazz blurted out. 'Why didn't you tell us?'

Auntie looked surprised. 'I was going to,' she replied. 'But then when you made it clear you didn't want me here, I thought you wouldn't believe me.'

'But you have to see things from our point of view,' Geena said carefully. 'We didn't want you because we thought we were doing all right and then you came and started interfering.'

'Oh, yes, I do realize that,' Auntie agreed. 'But when I saw how spoilt you all were—'

'Spoilt?' I echoed, shocked.

'Spoilt,' Auntie repeated coolly. 'I thought you needed a firm hand. I didn't realize at first that things weren't right. I went in with both feet flying. That's always been my problem.' She smiled ruefully. 'Mess things up first, regret it later.'

'That's just like Amber,' Geena remarked. 'It must run in the family.'

'Can we leave the personal insults for now?' I said.

Auntie looked faintly amused. 'And then things got worse, when you started trying to marry me off . . .'

We all blushed as one. 'You mean, you *know* about that?' Geena asked.

'Oh, yes,' Auntie said. 'Isn't that why you wanted me to meet your teacher, Amber?'

'Yes, but it didn't do much good, did it?' I shot back. I thought she'd had enough of the upper hand for the moment. 'You had a row with him.'

Auntie turned a delicate pink, which made me just a bit suspicious. 'Well, he annoyed me.'

'What did you argue about?' Jazz wanted to know.

'You three.' Auntie began to play with one of the gold bangles on her wrist. 'He wanted to help, but I was feeling touchy because I simply couldn't seem to get through to you.' She cleared her throat. 'It – er – just got out of hand.'

'He *is* very good looking,' I said innocently. 'Maybe you should meet him again and apologize.'

Auntie gave me a sharp glance, but all she said was, 'Well, perhaps I will. I was thinking that maybe I could get involved in your school PTA.'

Geena, Jazz and I flicked gleeful sideways glances at each other.

'That's a great idea,' I remarked. 'The PTA are always looking for parents who like interfer— I mean, helping out.'

The taxi driver wound down the passenger window. 'Hey, lady,' he called in a bored voice. 'Do you want this cab or don't you?'

Auntie regarded us thoughtfully. 'Well? Do I want it or not?'

'No, you don't,' said Geena. 'I think you should

184

come back and we should start over again.'

'Yes, I think we should,' Auntie agreed. 'We can see how we get on, at least.'

She got her suitcase out of the cab and paid the driver, who scorched off, doing a U-turn right across the middle of the crowded Broadway and earning himself more beeps and catcalls.

'I have to tell you,' Auntie went on, wheeling her suitcase along, 'that I do find it hard not to interfere. So I can't promise anything for the future.'

'That's all right,' I replied. 'We're not promising to be perfect either.'

'Oh no,' said Geena, sounding horrified.

'Definitely not,' Jazz agreed. 'We've had enough of that.'

Auntie smiled. 'Life should be very interesting, then, shouldn't it?'

'Oh, yes, I think so,' I said. 'Maybe now, while we're being all mature and adult, we can discuss my new trainers?'

WHAT WOULD JOEY DO?
Jack Gantos

'Joey Pigza, you need a life!'

Grandma wants Joey to find a friend, stop
running around after his nutty parents, and
start thinking about himself for a change.
But Joey's already got a life – a secret life as
Mr Helpful. Can this happy super-hero succeed
in his mission to keep everybody smiling?

'A must read'
Kirkus Reviews

'Funny but also heart-wrenching'
Booklist

ISBN 0440 865212